For
every
woman
who
has
had
enough

Anakana Schofield

na

FLEET
2020

FLEET

First published in Canada in 2019 by Alfred A. Knopf Canada
First published in Great Britain in 2020 by Fleet

1 3 5 7 9 10 8 6 4 2

A CIP catalogue record for this book is available from the British Library.

Hardback ISBN 978-0-349-72646-5
Trade paperback ISBN 978-0-349-72645-8

Book design by Kelly Hill
Interior images: (lightning bolt) © mhatzapa / Shutterstock.com;
(goat, kettle, bed) from 3,800 Early Advertising Cuts © Dover
Publications, Inc.; (glass) from Scan This Book © John Mendenhall

Printed and bound in Great Britain by Clays Ltd, Elcograf S.p.A.

Papers used by Fleet are from well-managed forests
and other responsible sources.

Fleet
An imprint of
Little, Brown Book Group
Carmelite House
50 Victoria Embankment
London EC4Y 0DZ

An Hachette UK Company
www.hachette.co.uk

www.littlebrown.co.uk

Bi

a novel in warnings

na

a novel in warnings

Bi

Also by Anakana Schofield:

MALARKY

MARTIN JOHN

I don't want to confirm myself in what I lived—in the confirmation of me I would lose the world as I had it, and I know I don't have the fortitude for another.

—CLARICE LISPECTOR,
The Passion According to G.H.

Her texts almost never coincide with the dates to which we refer, but they are pertinent, no matter how impertinent they may seem. We have our own methods of analysis and we ask you to kindly respect them, as we ask that you respect the unconscious work of our patient . . .

—LUISA VALENZUELA, *He Who Searches*

Index

Warnings

WARNING

I do swear.

In this place.

You will find.

Warnings.

If you heed them

They will be yours.

If you don't

You were warned.

My name is Bina and I'm a very busy woman. That's Bye-na not Bee-na. I don't know who Beena is, but I expect she's having a happy life. I don't know who you are, or the state of your life. But if you've come all this way here to listen to me, your life will undoubtedly get worse. I'm here to warn you, not to reassure you.

I am a modern woman with modern thoughts on modern things. I'm not a young person so I am used to being ignored. I expect you won't listen. The last time we met nobody listened to me.[1]

If you see me on the road and I pay no heed to you, know I have very good reasons for doing so. If you ever see a person lying in a ditch,[2] drive straight past them as fast as you can. And if a man comes to your door, do not open it.

These serve as my first two warnings.

No ditch.

No door.

---

[1] See, *Malarky: A Novel in Episodes.*

[2] Because I was reassured. He's a nice lad they said. He wasn't.

Do exactly as I tell you in matters mentioned here.
I have lived to tell this tale.
You could be a lot less lucky.

Ditch

Eddie is gone.

There is the son of Bina, the way there is the Son of God. His name is Eddie.

There is the Son of Satan, the way there is the Son of God. His name is also Eddie.

●

Eddie is a man.

Except Eddie is not Bina's real son.

He's her sorta son.

He managed to adopt himself onto Bina because she left her coat undone & in he climbed.

Latched + snatched.

That's Eddie.

●

Eddie's the kind of son you are landed with because no beggar wants to be bothered with him, and because he's used up all his goodwill and will soon expire on yours.

•

Bina lived a peaceful life.
Until she found Eddie
Landed in her ditch.
If she'd stayed indoors
She'd still be living a peaceful life.

•

Eddie is gone.
We give thanks that Eddie is gone.
We give thanks to God for that.

I didn't want him.

I didn't want to help him, but he presented in a manner that was impossible to ignore. Before I knew what I know now. Now I wouldn't help him. I won't help anyone. Not even you.

I'm only telling you this to warn you. I've better ways to waste my time than mithering on here. I'm a busy woman. Of that be certain. People think old women have nothing to do but stand around. They're very wrong and very ignorant and do take that last combination of wrong and ignorant as another warning. If people think you have time to stand about, let them know otherwise, by not standing about. Take off! Take off when they least expect it. *Could you just hold this for a minute?* Don't! Be gone. *Would you like to?* No. I wouldn't. *Can I borrow your bread knife to take on a picnic?* No. You can't. Because you'll never bring it back. *Would there be any chance . . . ?* No! There's no chance. None. None. None.

I will take exactly the time needed to tell my story & then it will stop. Any interruption or extension will not be my doing. It will be the undertakers or solicitors; whoever finds these papers and whoever it is decides on these things. Don't trust a word said after I've stopped. The final full stop will be in red. That's how you'll know.

Don't arrive at the end of this tale insisting it was too long or too wide or too unlike you. I am not interested in appealing to you. I am not you. I am only here to warn you.

We are all here because of legal reasons we probably cannot articulate without getting in trouble, but we will not burden each other by staying a page longer than is necessary. And there will not be a page more than absolutely is required. And if there is, write away and complain. There's probably an address to be found or a phone number. I won't care. Phone them all night long if you must. More likely you'll find a page missing. Or someone will have scratched out sentences or names in a thick black stripe. I'd better get going here fast before it happens.

Don't. Sign. Petitions. For. Me. You might see them around. I've heard about them. Ignore them. Read. This. Instead. You don't need 32,000 signatures to tell you anything as simple as what I'm going to tell you here. Yes I was wronged, but I was serviceably wronged because I've been handed this here undertaking. To. Deliver. These. Warnings. I am a practical woman, there's nothing I like more than to be useful and this here makes me useful. This serves only as a warning to you, if you are thinking of opening your hearth or your heart. Don't.

Of course I have better things to do, like making lists and learning hymns. I hate hymns but it's important not to stick out around here. If I stick out, I'll be lifted all over again[3] and all will be more terrible than it already is and was and might ever be. No one in a choir gets arrested. No one suspects people in choirs. Everyone's in a choir. That's why there's no one in jail anymore.[4]

Think slow and careful on that.

---

[3] I was arrested most recently in the shampoo aisle at Boots. I preferred being arrested at Shannon Airport. People thought I was being arrested for shoplifting in Boots. I wasn't. I never stole anything in my life.

[4] I know I was in jail for a week.

●

Bina found him in a ditch.
It was very annoying.
Quite the interruption
Especially for a Tuesday.
That was the first fella.
The young fella.
Eddie.

●

There are going to be two fellas I will warn you about.

Eddie's the first.

But the other fella.

There was another fella

Isn't there always another fella?

Where there's one, there's two.

He came to the door.

Civilized

On a Tuesday

Worry about the civilized types

On Tuesdays.

Ask yourself if someone highly clean & civilized is standing at your door, ask yourself what bold mischief that person could be capable of, then imagine it twice as bad. Imagine them taking a sword and lopping off your head, dragging a large knife down the front of you, opening you up like a shirt, spilling your giblets out on the road and rummaging through them. I generally find since I started doing this, it prompts me to shut my door as swift as I open it.

If the sword isn't working and your door is still open, imagine them taking a gun, a hunting rifle, the sort used to obliterate Bugs Bunny, and see yourself flung back against your airing cupboard peppered with fat bullets. This is what some fellas like to do to women. Don't let yourself be one of them.

Actually I'll put it direct: If they are knocking worry, worry about them. They are all after something. It might be something you do or don't have or are or aren't able for, but they can persuade you *they* are ready for it and so *you've* to be ready. Heed me on this. I've made every mistake you've yet to make and, if you're intent on not listening, are *about* to make.

And another thing, if someone asks you to put a bag over their head.

Don't do it.

They can change their mind.

That's what happened

The tall man.

Someone changed her mind.

A certain someone

I can't name.

Because of the courts.

In Castlebar.[5]

I shouldn't have named the place, but now I've no time to rub it out.

I have to carry on.

I'll have to give the tall man a name.

I'll call him the Tall Man.

I'll call him the Tall Man because I am in a hurry.

And to call him the Kettle Man sounds a bit funny.[6]

---

[5] I hate Castlebar. The radio described me as a Castlebar woman. "A Castlebar woman was remanded to custody this week charged with ███████." All kinds of unhelpful things are said on radios. I know. I listen to a lot of radio.

I am not a Castlebar woman. I hate Castlebar. They think they are Milan in Castlebar. They think they know better than the rest of us in Castlebar. I'd build a road straight through it. I'd flatten the place. I'd drop a bomb on it. OK Bina stop writing mad things you cannot scrub out. I do not mean it. The part about bombing Castlebar. I have no access to bombs. I wouldn't even know what one looked like. Put this page into the fire Bina. Stop adding to it. The trouble is I like what's on the other side of the paper. I can't tell you what it is, alright it's an ESB bill. I'm going to have to stick a piece of paper on top now to cover this part up. Castlebar brings out the worst in me. Second only to Eddie bringing out the absolute worst in me. I was in a charity shop there once & had to ask a man to shut up gossiping at the till. He turned & apologized & said he was only looking for directions to Tesco. I didn't turn since I was already facing him. I said what are you after at Tesco? You might find it here. I doubt it, he said. What are you after, I persisted. Windscreen fluid, roll-on deodorant for my wife & a pint of milk, he said.

[6] The first time he knocked at my door, I boiled the kettle & he eyed the games gathering dust on top of my cupboard & asked would I play Scrabble with him.

I am in a hurry because in case you didn't catch it earlier
I am a very busy woman.
If I write it out this way,
in these stacks,
you'll know I'm particularly in a hurry as I'm writing this bit.[7]

Someone is coming now so I'm going to hide it.

I'm back but I've forgotten where I was.
I'm in a hurry so I'll just carry on.
My memory isn't great so you may have to read a few things twice. What harm?
Nothing can be done about it.
Nothing to be done.
How it is when you are in a hurry.
I've to go on here until I am no longer or we'll never reach the red dot.

---

[7] Also, I might be writing it on the back of a receipt or a gas bill. Receipts aren't wide so to fit all the words on it they must be stacked. Receipts are easy to hide. And easy to come by. I have thousands of them despite having so little money to spend.

There's a thing about Eddie.
The thing about Eddie is he left.
The thing about Eddie is he's gone.
Everything about Eddie improved once he was gone.
That was the thing about Eddie.

There are a few more things about Eddie, but we'll get to
them yet.
If we have time.
If we've no time
You'll have to make do with what's above.
At any moment this could all stop.
Have I made that clear?

The ditch was the door.
One led on to the other

Led back to each other.
Brought us here to the warnings.
Where eventually we'll see the red dot.

When he's here, I worry about him.
When he's here, I can't stand him.
Yet when he's gone I just worry about him.
That's a relief.
But I can't stand worrying about him.
He's the ingrown toenail rubbing against your shoe.
You can't forget it's there.
You'll not forget Eddie's out there
Until finally you or he is not.
I'm here, I'm here, I'm here, he'd say.
I wish you weren't, I wish you weren't, I wish you weren't.

Eddie didn't give a fig about me though
Unless it was for money.
If it was money he needed, I was Eddie's number one.
I am still number one for money.

It would be worse if I were his mother—may the Lord have mercy on that poor, destroyed woman—God couldn't save her from Eddie. Eddie sent her to her grave. The way Eddie will surely send me to my grave. He'll send you to the grave too if you stand near him long enough. Hold him at arm's length. Go on push these papers out in front of you and count to twenty.

Don't.
Don't stand near him.
Easier now.
Now he's gone to Canada.
Pity the Canadians.
It'll take them a while to come around to him.
Then they'll ship him back to us.
I'll be gone by then.
I intend to be dead before I ever face that fella again.
Use this pile of papers as a weapon between you and Eddie.
Especially if he tries to kiss you.
Whatever you do put your hand across your mouth
He'll give you cold sores.
Hot burns.
Never learned.
Did Eddie.

For now he's quiet.
He's gone quiet.
I intend to be dead before Eddie is ever noisy again.

Have I already said that? Hard to keep track of what's said. People are always saying things I've never said. Exactly what I said to the first Judge. Hard to keep track, I said. Not a bit, he scowled. I won't forget his scowl. I shook my head at that scowl. I don't regret that. I'd do it again.

I have it planned this way. I've learned all I need to know about getting gone from the Tall Man. The instructions are in a box up there, cupboard over my head, near the front, easy to reach if you are reading this and finding me dead and looking for them. I am going to attach a note to the inside strap of my watch to make it easy for you to locate them. The tiny sticker will read c u p b o a r d

I always found fellas very difficult. I never got tangled up in them for that reason. I put my head down and lived a reasonable life. Or rather *once* I put the head down, I lived a reasonable life.

Women are no easier. So don't be fooled thinking otherwise.

They are all awful, awful, awful.

All humans are awful.

All of us are awful.

Be very suspicious.

Stick to cats or carp.

Goats are less trouble than humans.

He's mad as a goat, they'll say. Yet I never met a goat as mad as a man.

Goats never caused me mounds of grief.

Goats never sat like a pile of rank mush in my kitchen.

Worse thing they ever did was eat something they couldn't digest, yet you'd no more go down their throat after it. You leave them be. You let them decide, do you want to live or die? Do you want to carry on or take a left turn?

A man though, he could get into your kidneys and irritate them & you in a very special way. It's why women are up in the night to go to the toilet as they age. They are widdling the confused strain of anger gathered up in there all day. I've no explanation as to why men are up piddling all night too, except perhaps it's God's subtle way of tormenting them. He goes straight for the pipe does our Saviour.

Out of the toilet quick, Bina!

Before I'm distracted.

I'm an awful woman for distraction.

Curiosity was my downfall.

You'll see yet.

But let us return to the goats.

Not demanding, goats.

Unless they sneak out.

Then and even then, and only then, it's the humans cause a big fuss. The goats don't much mind the humans; they carry on doing what they do, a simple desire to eat briars unimpeded. Armoured tongues. Clipping nibbles. Head in. Chomp crunch. Down. Down. You could be dying on the ground and a goat would eat all the way around you, and not take a lick or a bare sniff at you. He'd follow the feed.

Not the humans! Oh no, big fuss when goats escape. They're out on the road! Mad. Arms waving. Phones ringing. Thumb-stabbing slipped texts to the wrong farmer. They raise their voices. They'll shout at any man who'll hear. Any ear. Or woman. And amid shrieking carnival and lifeboat dispatch you'd wonder wherever did they think goats were before we put them into fields and sheds? Where do they think the wild goats are? The goats just keep on eating and buck about. They don't mind your trumpet or your texts.

I've had to give up my goats on account of the humans. Let me be clear on that, it wasn't the other way round. I haven't given up my goats for any reason aside from Eddie. Don't listen when they say *oh it's her age or her health* or *the diabetes* or *she needs to lose weight.* I haven't the diabetes. It's Joanie, God rest her, who had the diabetes. None of us knew. She kept it quiet and now she's dead and that's what happens when you keep things quiet. Though I do believe in keeping some things quiet. Phil had it too, the diabetes.[8]

I am as strong as steel. Unbendable Bina. It's just the humans are doing me in. Not the goats, not the diabetes. I don't even eat cakes. If I start eating cakes, it's because they drove me to it. Eddie would drive you to eat cakes. I'm surprised I didn't plunge my face down into a Victoria sponge, with him and now this other tall fella breaking my brain to crumb.

---

[8] See, *Malarky: A Novel in Episodes.*

There has to be a plan. I'll have to kill the cat if I'm to go. That's a pity. For the best. Nice cat though. Except when it piddled all over the place early on. Including on my new pillows, because Eddie locked the poor *craytur* in my bedroom. Them's the sort of stupid thing Eddies do.

I didn't want it to get out, he said.

You locked him in my bedroom for two days and gave him no food because you didn't want him to get out?

He didn't get out tho', he said.

He couldn't get out! He was locked in!

That cat's not dead, said he. As if there were some fear the cat would be dead if it lived a normal cat's life.

It's very hard to get run over when you are locked inside my bedroom.

Most cats die. Most cats let out die. They die on the road.

And he believes it. He holds fast. Plain, dry, seasoned oblivious. Smothered with fungal oblivion. He could live, die and rise again entirely oblivious that man. Every time the thought revisits me that I should have left him in that ditch. I am thinking it as I write this to you. I'm warning you not to lift men out of ditches and don't trust the common declaration "all he needs is a bang on the head." Eddie received a big bang on the head when he landed off his motorbike in my ditch and there is no evidence of it improving him. I don't know how I didn't take the cat and brain him with it. Except the poor creature had suffered enough. My pillows never recovered and the smell of cat piss still lingers. It's a reminder. Heed your reminders. Your mistakes always come with reminders. Often there's a smell of a reminder. Log it. Sniff it. Choke on it. Make your nose passport and border control. Let no one in.

Since Eddie's gone, I've put items in his bed to remind myself he is gone. But I had to throw out the mattress,[9] the pillows and sheets he'd slept on for years, because he was filthy anytime he lay down on them. You could never wash the smell of him away. I've one room stinks of cat's piss and another of Eddie. I hesitated though, because according to my prophecy I thought the smell of him could, if I left it, serve as a warning. I'm happy to say I'm past needing a warning, which is why I am able to batter this out to yourselves. I've transcended.

I often wonder at the women who give birth to awful young fellas like Eddie. I think there's a case to be heard for shoving the likes of Eddie back up and starting all over again. I believe in abortion since I met Eddie. It's only a shame you can't abort a 40-year-old.

I believe in obliteration. I believe in removing useless specimens from the planet. I don't say it aloud, but I'm committed.

---

[9] I wonder now if I hadn't had the delay on needing to get a new mattress might I have saved Phil. Maybe, in the end, Eddie will have killed the pair of us without even trying.

You can only say it aloud if God has told you to do it. He hasn't, but On My Oath if I were called I would serve. Likewise, I believe that the more useful amongst us should also have some choice about when we go. That is why I joined the Group when the Tall Man came to my door.

Eddie's gone quiet now.
So we are waiting. That's all I do now.
Wait.
Suspiciously.
Primed.

What kind of a strange place is Canada if they let Eddie in?
Maybe they don't know he's in.
I won't tell them.
They can keep him.
He's theirs.
Sometimes they send them back.
I don't want Eddie back.
Maybe I'll phone the embassy and register
He's not mine and I don't want him.

I rang the embassy

There was a bit of confusion

You don't need a visa, the woman said

I'm not after a visa, I said

I'm in bed and I won't be going anywhere.

I was going to tell her I was arrested.

I decided to tell her.

I was arrested, I said.

Was I Canadian?

Not a bit, I said. I was never there in my life. I only saw an advert for it on the television.

I'm calling about a fella you've let in there.

The line went dead.

I waited.

Hold for consulate services, said she.

And a phone rang and a recorded woman's voice said she was Daphne and not at her desk.

I thought it was a bit silly, telling that.

If someone wanted to rob her they'd know now was a good time to do it.

I left her a message.

Daphne, I said, You don't know me and I am ringing you anonymous about a man who is over there and if ever you send him back, no matter what he says, don't send him back to me. I hung up. I felt much better.

That finally I had said to someone he's not to come here.

If I said it once, I could say it again.

I was grateful to Daphne for listening to it.

I started thinking a lot about Canada and what kind of people might be there, and would there be any hope they'd beat Eddie over the head?

I didn't like their Prime Minister, he was flighty. He looked like he'd take off if he went rolling up an escalator too fast. But he'd a good coat on him. I don't like our Prime Minister. He's an awful man. I can't remember his name but he's very hairy ears. A bit like a wolf. I'll be honest I'm only repeating what a woman I delivered Meals on Wheels to said about him, because I'm not much for television. Her name was Mary and one day out of nowhere she said, would you look at the ears on him. She was pointing at the television claiming it was the Taoiseach. I didn't have the heart to tell her it was actually a badger and now I'm after repeating the story myself without remembering the woman was confused. She was angry about something, I forget what. I agreed with what she was angry about. For I'm angry about a lot of things and I've no one agreeing with me at all.

That's a warning. Two even.

Find someone who'll agree with you.

Don't repeat stories about people on the television.

Life is nothing but ordeals.

Have you noticed?

There are ordeal creators.

That's a fact.

Eddie's one.

One Eddie is too many.

Anytime I hear that name I take a jolt. There was a dog passing recent and I thought I heard a voice call out Eddie. I ran inside and hid in my bed. Literally pulled the covers up over my head. I said to myself that dog'll kill you if you stay out another three seconds. And I waited. I waited to hear Eddie's gorsy tones. Nothing. That was when I realized Eddie had gone to my head. That I was suffering in his absence.

The next day, though, was a Wednesday and I woke up with sense again.

I recovered. I was glad that Eddie was gone.

Long may he stay that way.

I wouldn't want him dead tho'

Because it might be up to me to bury him

And it would be an awful lot of work

And I'm not for another funeral for a while.

Except, obviously, my own.

That's a bit glum.

But that's what a man like Eddie will do to you.

He'd make you glum.

Especially on a Tuesday.

Watch Tuesdays. Careful on Tuesdays. They are very dangerous days.

Hard on the head.

If you're a man called Eddie reading this: Change your name. Say you are Sam or Tom.

Door

I will say that I was surprised when this other fella came to my door one night and asked me a question. This is the Tall Man I talk of, not Eddie. Eddie is squat and pouchy. I am getting old now and my memory is dotted but I still remember being surprised that a man with a question was standing at my door.[10]

He was an unremarkable man. That's all I recall of him. It was dark, remember. It is also a dark remember, so I need to get this written out quick, lest I lose my courage to record it. He may have worn a long coat. Could he be lost, or a preacher, or collecting for charity? Those were my first thoughts. He was neither. He was, I see now, just another man content to put me in a whole pile of trouble. I swear there's a factory out there producing them for the task. There's probably 54 already minted and I've another 52 coming for me yet.

What was it he wanted again? Wait now. How can I say it without actually saying it.

---

[10] Because I am a woman full of questions, I never expect even more of them to arrive at my door. Or men to arrive at my door with them.

What he wanted me to do eventually[11] became a mountain of woe and had me sent inside prison for a week. I didn't like the food. It was glop and stodge and unrecognizable. Every single item was the colour of porridge or covered in breadcrumbs. Except the jam. The jam was orange only because it was marmalade. But the young people were good to me. They shuddered and said wrong, it was all wrong, all wrong Bina and I shouldn't be in there and I didn't disagree with them. I shrugged. I enjoyed it because, even though it was prison, it was still a week's holiday from Eddie. But then I started to have very bad dreams they'd hang me in there. I didn't like the tin toilets and you weren't allowed to use talc.

Eddie, it turned out, was an acorn of trouble in comparison to this Tall Fella at the door. I believe he's hiding out in England now, the Tall Man.[12] Very unfair. He was only trying to help. It wasn't his fault that someone changed their mind and told their daughter.

---

[11] Because it didn't stop here. It never stops where it starts. Just like Eddie. I was only helping him for a few weeks until I was lumbered with him (for 10 years) until he decided to flee.

[12] You didn't hear that from me. Not to be repeated beyond these papers if you don't mind.

Never have a daughter, they report on you and get into your knicker drawer and shift things around. Never have a son either. They don't get into your knicker drawer but they are clowns. They drive drunk. They don't change their jumpers. They only have half-witted answers and they eat everything in the house. They'd even eat raw lard. And they are never out of the toilet. Clowns. Pure Clowns. And there's better ways to waste your time than with clowns.

Joanie's daughters ruined her funeral. That's a fact. Maybe that's why Phil suddenly wanted gone. I wouldn't do that one. She was on her own with that. Too risky. We might have even been buried together if we'd both had enough on the same Sunday. Don't mind me. I didn't say that, but I haven't time to rub it out so it'll have to stand.

I have given you several facts so far.

Add them up and I might give you a prize to send away for at the end. Mind, I've become very bitter about prizes, I've sent away for 200 of them and I only ever won a mobile phone and I didn't like it and it's still in the box because the plug was missing when I opened it.

After Eddie what you'll remember
Before Eddie what you'll forget
Between Eddie what you'll never understand.[13]

If I were to write a eulogy for Eddie, you have just read it.

We don't know what's to come. We don't know what's ahead and avoidance should be our only objective by the time you are finished reading this. If there's anyone reading it? If there isn't I am only wasting my time but at least I'm lying down wasting it. And at least he's gone. If he's at your door, I warned you. There's only so much a woman can do. Lie down and issue warnings. There are other places to issue them these days, so don't hold back.

Lamp posts are good.

Car windows.

The internets.

Tell people.

Unless they are moles.

Don't tell moles anything.

Women can be moles too.

---

[13] Avoid him in the hereafter.

Bina lived a peaceful life
Until she found Eddie in her ditch.
If she'd stayed inside her curtains
Bina'd still be living a peaceful life.

Also, don't answer the door. Don't answer the door if there's a tall man standing there.[14] Some tall men are nice tall men and some tall men are just a bucket of trouble.

Even if you need something heavy lifted don't let them in. Let it stay where it is.

Leave the men on the mat.

Where you can get a proper look at them.

Because once they are sitting down . . .

Well everyone improves guzzling your tea.

Don't forget.

You can't tell by looking at them.

Especially if you're distracted and there's something inside boiling on the cooker.

Like an egg hopping uncomfortable inside a pot.

---

[14] Always ignore strange noises
Unless someone has left their Kenwood mixer on.
Leave troubled men be
But don't ruin the dough.
Don't let fine dough be ruined.

They catch you weak and they're in.
You remember the egg.
Oh come in for a minute.
Never do it.
Risk the egg.
Rather than let the rasher across your mat.
That was another warning
See
Men stay on the mat
Don't let them in
In means din.

I am ready to write the manual. I am going to write a combat manual. This might even be it. I think it's time women prepared for war on the doormat. I don't agree with women wearing pyjamas though. I am strange that way. I've never been comfortable with them. I don't like the waists on them. You couldn't put a gun in them without someone seeing.

I don't have a gun, but if I did I'd put it in my pocket.

Now I've the socialists, the Marxists, the laryngists and the mangle-ists signing permissions and petitions to free me. But I am not locked up. They are outside camping with their clipboards, in case the Guards come for me, and to be honest now, they are in my way and I wish they'd shift off my land. Eddie made a big mess up on that land & someone could lose their life tripping over it. I didn't ask them to come and they give me no choice. Uninvited, every day they are out there making videos of the top of my head while I am doing the washing up. They've installed an extension cord through my kitchen window and I've had to unplug my clock radio while they charge whatever it is they are charging out there. I do not know where it is they are shitting and piddling and I don't ask.

They say they'll chain themselves to me if anyone comes. I told them to think of no such thing, that I am not a bovine and if anyone comes for me they're welcome to me. They laughed light and said you're a gas woman, and offered me some strange dried peas I wouldn't feed to a pig. I tried to say again I'm not a gas woman. I only wish everyone would cease inquiring and pass on without comment. I am not the Ukraine, I said. I don't need defending. Would that they listen to what I am saying and leave me the hell alone in peace. No. They will not. Won't and don't and carry on insisting I'm a symbol and they keep referring to people I've never heard of. Rita. Rita so and so, she's serving 13 months for something. It's you and Rita, they quo-spout. And how old is Rita, say I by reply. She's

30. Do I look 30 to you? Even if they try to lock me up for 30 years, I'll be dead in 10. But, oh they're all socialist, Marxist, dig in with their class war, petrol, gas pipeline, price of fuel, right to turf, capitalist, bigamist, polyagony and, probably, if I listened close enough, primping and pimping. And who is listening to them? I'll tell you who. 39 stars above and a half-deaf badger exhausted from the noise off them. They might as well shout into a drain. I might prefer common criminals if they said less. They do their damage and they're gone. They might kill you dead, but they don't bore a hole in your brain. They aren't boring and you don't get a wet head in the rain listening to them.

Lookit, I've told them straight I want no one killed, I want no one pregnant and I want no one piddling on my land and I'd rather you'd all be gone by tomorrow. They nod. They nod like there is nobody home, yet they're agreeing that there is. They use words like privilege and resistance and this kind of head-bangy-arsy-varsy that takes a long time to cross the tongue and there's always something on the cooker and back inside I go, distracted and disgruntled, until again they are at me with the phones filming the top of my head and do I have anything to say about my situation?

I do. Oh God I do. Would you fuck off outta my way.

Instead, out the window I cheerfully spit

Carry on with your lives now lads, otherwise I might be glad of a spell in prison and a bit of rest from the lot of ye.

And every time I hang out the washing, there's seven of them looking at me and three of them leaping to help and I tell them straight: At my age, I know how to hang out washing. I've hung out washing twice as long as you've been alive!

I've warned them if I keep finding them under my armpit I'll personally check myself + the lot of them into prison for trespass and we can be stuck together in a cell and there will be no commute required. They put up the palms in retreat and back off and for a few days I am left to myself unimpeded until, like the cheeky cat next door coming to snifflelickspit on food that's not his, in they sidle all over again to give me reports. Reports! We think you should know . . . we're ready to defend you should anything go down. Go down! Would there be any chance a passing dose of plague might come down and remove the lot of them and could it do me this useful favour in the next 30 minutes, right after this cup of tea.

I told them
Already.
No fuss, I told them,
I can have no fuss here.
Because fuss could bring Eddie back.
We don't want Eddie back.
I'd take prison over Eddie.
They want to know. Who's Eddie?
They'll sort him.
They'll protect me.
We'll get Eddie.
We'll get him.
He's ours!
We're yours!

Suffering Jesus, I tell them I can't even hear that man's name, would you keep your voice down. I don't want protecting, I don't want Eddie, I just want to be left in peace. But never are they convinced or convincible, only keep saying I mustn't feel I am taking advantage of them, because they *want* to be here and they'll stand up to this government and these gangster crooks, like the ESB or ECB and the TSB. Every time they seem to change the letters on me. I like the TSB and I told them this. I like them at Easter, I said. I went in there once and a man gave me a doughnut. No, that wasn't the TSB, they say. The TSB is digging up Nigeria, they say. The TSB is doing all kinds of bad things to mammals and kerbs and they're eating tires and beating clouds and imprisoning pandas. And that wasn't a doughnut they gave you. What? It was a doughnut. It had jam in it! Bitumen they shout. Tar! Oil! Gas! What? I think I am going to pass out, I say. Get her a chair, says that lanky lang. Don't touch me. Stop talking so loud. All of you shut up fighting in my ear. They apologize and whisper and say they didn't mean to upset me. Go on, you're alright, I relent. Then I usually have them carry up a bucket of turf. Because they need something else to think about other than bitumen.

There's a new fella out there, the lanky looper I call him, with a thin face and a long beard that might have food gone relic inside it. He has it twisted down to a point and a red elastic band put on it with a bead or three, and he looks surgically demented. I don't care what you put on yourself. I wouldn't care if you tattooed a droopy spider on your baldhead like a lampshade, but a grown man with three pink beads hanging from his chin is disturbing. There's just nothing right about it. And it's not a nice thought, but when he is bitumen-ing on, I have considered grabbing the dangle and yanking it off him very hard, one strong pull and handing it blithely back with the whispered words, sorry, there was something stuck on your chin and it was distracting me.

That's a very dark thought.

No wonder I am being locked up.

I don't remember—had I such dark thoughts when I'd a man living here within my gaze, who if the forces that be had flattened him dead, I would have cheered? That's not a dark thought, that's a truthful thought and I don't care who you tell it to. I would warn you never to disclose your dark thoughts but to constantly disclose your truthful thoughts, because it's only the dark ones that follow when the truthful ones are hid.

It's very hard to do anything with these young Crusties spying on me. Every time I go into the loo, I see the shadow of a head or shade of a herd of heads passing up and down the path outside. I can't even burp loudly because they'll hear me and write it down and send it to Vincent Browne or one of these men on the TV and the radio who never shut up all day and are scruffy looking. If I were on the TV, and as rude as he can be, I'd at least take a bath and I'd at least do up my shirt and I'd think about the poor people who've to listen and look at me. People like me, stuck with Eddie. All over this country, there are people waking up day by day beside people they are disappointed to discover aren't dead. I don't care. I'm going to say it. You can think what you will. It's factual talk. And this government deciding they've to carry on living with them. And they wonder why the murder rate is so high. And them's the ones they are catching. I don't want to imagine the number they are not.

The Crusties have gone mad, patrolling. They take turns to plod up and down, like border guards. They record it in books. They film each other walking up and down my path. Even the hens are confused. It's worse than North Korea in my garden. The path is thin. One twisted his ankle. At first they held walkie-talkies! Imagine what a thing! Turn them off, I told them. You're wasting your batteries. There's nothing happening here. You never know, they said. I do know, I said, I know all too well because the one thing happening here has already happened. It was 10 years of Eddie and I wanted him gone and the only use for this patrolling is to alert me should he ever come back, so I can immediately run out this door and jump straight into the lake.

See amn't I smart now.

I never offered one among them a cup of tea.

I never offered a towel nor the use of my toilet.

See how I heed the warnings now

See how finally I paid heed to my own warnings.

Which is the only good use for them

Other than writing them here.

For you to ignore
At your peril.

I did a bold thing.
I am going to whisper it.
It wasn't a particularly nice thing to do
But I did it anyway.
I'm not advising you to do it.
I'm not publicly advertising this.
I am merely recording it here
Between us
As done.

OK.
I admit it.
I phoned the radio.
Told them I was a prisoner inside my own home.
I've a vanful of Crusties out there.
Camping, I said.
The researcher said it was strange

Aggressive, I said.

They've swarmed me.

Do you know them?

I do not.

And didn't they come down and interview them.

And didn't they splice all their voices together.

And didn't a pile of people come the whole next day from the vicinity

To get a look at them.

And didn't the Crusties become very excited

And think it was time for a pitched battle.

Wrapped their faces in dirty tee-shirts

Like they were fighting for Chechnya.

And didn't I go out there and tell that young fella waving a lump of wood that if he didn't put it down I'd put it up him.

And didn't the whole thing end up in the newspaper.

And there was I only aiming for the radio.

Finally TG4 turned up because, of course, they would have to have an Irish speaker out there like the Buddha of the encampment. Earnest in two languages.

He is the awful one who plays the bongo drums and can't sing in tune.

I swear I'd like to murder him.

They knocked at the front door

With the television camera

And that Big Number 4

Under the lack of a chin.

Have you any statement, Chinless said.

He was small

With a Donegal accent.

Idir dhá teanga.
Yes, I said.
I kept it short.
I'd like to murder them, I said
And shut the door.

And by Christ, even though they dubbed me *as Gaeilge* on the *Nuacht*, it set them phoning. There was no one who didn't phone. The only call I answered was the Solicitor. Stop it, he said. Stop saying you want to murder people. You're going to scupper us all if you keep this up. There is no us, I thought. There's just me. Last I checked there are no double berths for the convicted and their solicitors in any prison in this country.

There's only one man I want to murder and he's in Vancouver, I said. That's the only thing I have to say on this matter.

I put down the phone.

And that was the point. The point was or is, in the very matter itself. I forget the point. I forget the was or is. What is the point? Merciful hour, how this keeps happening to me. A name, a word, a meaning, a person, it's all unthreading and blowing out the backdoor of my mind. I'm fading to remember why I do the things I do and who is at war with whom. The only memory I unfortunately cannot seem to unthread is Eddie's forty-gutted face. Ah that's it, there's the point: Where were all these people when and while I was boxed in here for lengthy years with Eddie?

Where were you and you and you?

Where was him and her and she and he?

Where was this hillock full of bearded bandits tripping up and over my hens?

Why didn't they descend on me then?

Then was when I needed them.

Then was when

They'd have been useful.

And, in trying to relieve myself of that image of boots clipping my hen's wing, when I think further on it, who was it had knocked at my door? Why only the Tall Man. Only he came useful, bearing sufficient distraction to occupy me and enable me to escape Eddie. I had him and I'd Phil. Only when the Tall Man was sat here at this table did I have a moment's peace from Eddie. Only then did Eddie evict himself, even temporarily. Only Dr Death, as the papers have labelled him since, could silence the dodo, who's so slippery not even the papers, despite trying, can catch up with him. For it wasn't that long after the Tall Man made my acquaintance that Eddie set up the yard, which at first appeared a change for the better.

What looks to be a change for the better initially, can, if carefully and sceptically observed, be an unambiguous deep slide into the dire.

Keep your eye sharp.

Make no decision about what anything might be or become until the very worst of it is upon you.

Don't. Invite. Change.

Don't imagine things change for the better.

They don't.

If he's awful like Eddie assume he'll remain that way.

Unless unconscious.

Eddie was pleasant enough up in the ICU in Castlebar hospital.[15]

He was bearable with his eyes closed and in a coma.

Carry on with burdensome people only if you enjoy having something to moan about.

Otherwise hammer your expectation towards the tin can of inevitable failure.

Tin is tin.

Tin's din.

Let din in and he'll only give you more tin.

███████ from the Group phoned. Stop it, she said. Don't use words like murder. It is the wrong kind of attention, she said. It's going to damage our work. You're important, she said. We couldn't do it without you. He (she speaks of the Tall Man) trusts you the most and there's others waiting and needing us.

I agreed I'd stop. I'll stop, I said, if you can get these slugs out of my back garden and keep me out of prison.

Go out.

Go out?

Go out, she said, and say you'd *respectfully appreciate* it if

---

[15] After I very foolishly retrieved him out of my ditch.

they'd all leave. That you appreciate their enthusiasm, but they are disrupting your life.

Very good, I said

I'll do that.

I put down the phone and I worried. I worried about going out. She was right. She was wrong. She was half right. She was not a bit right. She was a full turn and a half wrong. Say I went out and one was to sneak in here, it'd be Eddie all over again. I know squatters. 40 minutes on a rug and it's theirs. No court can shift them. 2 hours in your bed and they possess your life. I looked at a man down in a ditch and 10 years of my life was ruined. And it would probably be the worst among them who'd slip in. It would be that bacon-faced bongo drummer, that recently converted gaeilgeoir, and he'd never stop addle-prattling about my pronunciation and that would be in English, never mind Irish, and we'd have Eddie all over again, but in two languages all day long. The more I thought of going out, the more I shrunk back in. No No No. No way. No how. No, *would you?* No, *appreciate.* No, *respectfully.* Never *respectfully appreciate.* No, nothing of the sort. Only shift your furry arses before I insert something into them and hop you all off to Mars. But no, see now I didn't do that either. I put the electric blanket on and into the bed I went, even though the hallway clock said it was only half four.

Defeated.

Defeated again by clowns.

Factory-made ones.

Made in the boreens of Spiddal.

Budded in Buncrana.

Smelt very bad since leaving Salford.

Now come here to invade me.

I woke starved at midnight after very bad David Bowie dreams. His face was half penguin and half blue. He was fully penguin on the bottom. Yet he was wearing yellow tights and nothing on his top half, but he'd no wings. How could he be wearing yellow tights if he was penguin on the bottom? It's why I do not like waking from bad dreams. I'll have to scratch that out. Should I lose the yellow or the penguin? Which will perturb you less? No matter. I've no warning to share over David Bowie dreams.

If you have them, you'll grow into them.

Fact.

But never in my life, and it was a sheltered enough life til I imported Eddie into it, have I had such visitations. I've sympathy for people caught unawares by visits from saints. I would never be right near a grotto again.

Oh plenty.

Sure I'd plenty, plenty dreams.

I'd had swallowing-chewing-gum dreams, falling-down-a-well-and-breaking-my-neck dreams, forgetting-where-I-live dreams, on-my-holidays-in-Rome dreams, catching-a-too-bigfish-that-pulled-me-into-the-sea dreams, I'd had them all. But never a pop star in transition to the aquatic wearing yellow tights. I opened the back door in an attempt to dissolve the images and was gasping as I shut it. The numb nail lords had lit a fire on top of where I'd buried four ducks six years ago. Eddie had a role in their deaths. He reversed a trailer over the poor creatures, who thought and assumed they were napping safely inside the enclosure I had them living in. Eddie blamed me and said I needed an outside light. I remember the exchange. I came out of the house with my angry arms aloft. He continued reversing. I screamed at him. He continued reversing. I attempted to place myself between the ducks and his reversing. He opened the door.

What are you doing?

You are on the ducks, I said. Get off the ducks.

What's that, he said, I can't hear you.

Get off the fucking ducks. You've killed them dead!

He tried to insist it was the only route and it took another 90 seconds of cursing at him before he drove forward and turned the monster off. He walked a few steps and stared. Fuck, he said. I told you to put in an outside light. Then I let out an anguished growl and called him a murderer. And that he was not to cross my mat until he had cleaned up the carnage he had created.

Later he did apologize. Not to me. He said he felt sorry for the ducks and that if he hadn't squashed them so bad we could have put them in a pot like the Chinese do and eat them. I resolved to dispose of them myself for fear they could suffer further and he might try to sell them to a takeaway because that is how stupid he was. Sure enough I found he'd put them in individual carrier bags and when I opened them he'd taken their heads off with the axe. Dismal. Dismal. Dismal. Dismal. I took care instead to give them a proper burial spot and I surrounded it with lumps of brick so no eejit could drive over it without first bursting his tires. And this circle of bricks is, I must suppose, why these Crusties designated it their fire pit.

I had to go up and confront them. They were going to torch the ducks' bones. If I'd wanted them made ashes I'd have lit them on fire myself.

I will say one thing: as I stood outside dithering about going up, it was clear that I could no longer take assertive decisions the way I once could. Suspiciously, as soon as Eddie left I lost whatever small courage I had.

The realization I was lacking the basic courage to walk outside my door and confront a gang of misery-making, uninvited do-gooders propelled me and my poker back indoors to drop down into the chair beside my solid-fuel range. Nothing remarkable to say about it. (I can't afford oil. Fierce expensive.) It leaks smoke and it's nothing but a punishment to live beside. It was not a comfortable landing as there was a telephone directory and three damp towels left on the chair. The corner of the directory hit sharp an area of my body I will not be disclosing and caused me to rise as hurriedly as I'd sank. I helicoptered about, more useless foostering, until I made my way back to bed still hungry. Hungry and now more confused than David Bowie's visit could ever make me. There's nothing quite as confusing as yourself, I concluded. This is likely why so many of us succumb to absolute confusion, the dementia, in the end.

Another woman.

A woman not in a hurry.

The way I am in a hurry here.

Such a woman, she'd lay herself back in the bed at this point in the proceedings and disclose every thought that followed the laying back, down onto this paper. She'd lace up paragraphs that would absorb you and you'd believe her, because you're easy this way.[16] I am not that woman. I'm not easy. I might dither about the dark, about the destruction of my ducks' final resting spot, but I won't dither here. I won't fill up this page with false recollections of important thoughts I've never had. You'll have to make those ones up. I'm busy here. Busy trying to report what's actively being lived whether you like that or not.

It's how it is.

And you never like how it is.

It's why you read in the first place.

Isn't it a pity about you, for how am I to warn you if I'm not to tell you how it is?

---

[16] I saw this when I was arrested. I saw how simple the thinking on right and wrong is and how there's no road found in between.

Plain. I lay down.

Simple. I was miserable.

Fact. If I can't get rid of them Crusties outside and I am forever inside worried about the return of Eddie.

Surely

My time is up.

It's time to be gone.

They've boxed me in

Both-eared in two time zones.

This is what they do if you don't heed the warnings.

Warnings I'd plenty.

Plenty gone unhed.

Plenty gone that is.

Me the unheeder

Now instructing you, the unheeded.

Oh pot kettle, pot kettle pot, kettle pot pot.

I noticed it got very popular

Blaming the church

On the radio.

You could blame the church all day long

Then turn the dial

And start blaming them all over again.

I decided to do likewise and blame the church for Eddie.

Since he's gone,

Eddie's been ringing.

He leaves strange messages.

About needing help.

Never asks how I am.

Every message begins the same way

He tells me who he is (as if I have forgotten)

And he says

So I need[17] you to . . .

He closes every message with the words *God Bless.*

I find that most annoying.

More annoying than him not asking how I am.

More annoying than him asking me for help (read: money).

God Bless.

Bless what?

Good riddance to God.

He blessed me with Eddie.

Every message is more annoying than the last.

If I wanted to be rude I'd say *annoying like the gospels.*

But I am not rude.

Eddie's rude.

That's what Eddie would say.

---

[17] See how it's a command not a request he leaves on my answering machine.

She's more annoying than the gospels, he used to say about me and people would look at him strange and offer no reply. So he'd have to repeat it. Someone should have told him to shut up, but that's the problem with men like Eddie, nobody is saying what needs saying. And wait now til you hear how suddenly he wasn't such a bad lad. And wait now til you hear how it was only since he left that I lost the run of myself. And I must miss him. Rather than the truth. NOT A BIT. Not even a porridge-sized bit. Not a crumb. As a fella once said to me from the front of his car, if you tell people the truth they won't believe you, but tell them lies and they'll believe all of it.

I am seeing this now. I am seeing this here today. I am seeing it in the court system, which has me captured while that lug is set free and gone to Canada.

And that is one of the many reasons why I am here warning you.

I have done things people asked me to do because they needed doing.

I was not supposed to do those things.

I have lost all my courage now.

It is a shame that.

That was a warning.

Don't do the things you're not supposed to do.

Even if people ask you to do them.

Don't.

See now when Eddie phones and leaves the recurring message that he needs me to send him money.

I press erase.

It takes practice, but it's possible.

Eddie's phoned-in requests are varied.

From the basic:

    —Rent.

    —I need to buy a phone.

    —I can't phone you if I've no phone (even as he's
      phoning me)

To the vague:

    —In a bit of bother

    —Just need it til next Thursday

To the outright false:

    —Root canal

    —I have a girl pregnant

    —Need to go to a funeral.

    —Have broken my foot.

The man is a lying hoar. He has lied far and wide and double-eared for 10 years.[18] He'll lie til the pyramids are fully eroded and rebuilt in Lego.

He'll fib on into the 70th century that fella.

Erase.

Heed me.

Erase him and all of them.

Erase. Erase. Erase.

Then into bed.

Take to the bed.

Only place they can't wreck your head.

Good woman.

If I do nothing else in these warnings, I will train you to say no.

You'll be howling No! No! No! back at them, because I'll drill this down here so often it'll infect you.

Practise.

Form your lips and shoot a big nooooh out of them.

Chomp them forward and let it blow.

Then rapid-fire 33 short ones.

---

[18] And these are only the years I know about . . .

No. No. No. No. No. No. No. No. No. No. No. No. No.
No. No. No. No. No. No. No. No. No. No. No. No.
No. No. No. No. No. No.

This is what no rapid-fired 33 times looks like.

I have not and am unlikely to ever figure out how to do the follow-up part, which ensures they know not to ask. Never to ask. Never to dare to ask. Also, there are many for whom ears shut on hearing the word no. No matter how much you practise. No matter if you bellow, hoard or howl it. No matter if you're crying. No matter if you're bleeding. No matter if you're wounded.

That's unreasonable.

For some of them though, if required, I recommend you add the words: I'll have you shot.

Say it simple, but say it like you are very capable of making that happen. Use your domestic breeding to deliver it. Say it like you're telling the person you need to take something out of the oven. Go on, whisper it over to them now.

I had to say it once and sometimes it's only the once it needs to be said.

You know what words are not unreasonable.
I have had enough.
I have had enough and I know this to be a fact.
You'll know when you've had enough
You'll know when you know this to be a fact.
And when you do it's a perfectly reasonable thing

And in the cases I am thinking of, where I have had people confide it to me, I have chosen to believe them. I do not dissuade anybody of the facts they claim to know about themselves, unless they are useless facts up to no good or they concern aliens. I'm not for aliens. But I do not believe that the Gardai, the government or any other human necessarily knows better than the human herself when she has had enough.

If you tell me you've had enough, I will believe you.

Eddie came off the drink.
He came off the drink on a Tuesday
And everything got worse.
She had no concept he'd be worse off it than on it.

██████████ from the Group phoned and said I still had the Exit bags. I had all the bags and they needed to get them back.

You'll have to come and get them, I said. I can't leave.

The house is probably being watched, she said.

We'll have to think about it.

Think about it.

You haven't misread.

Eddie became worse off the drink than on it, she's telling you.

Be careful what you wish for.

That's harsh.

But this hasn't been a difficult book yet.

Bina's not for difficult books.

Life is full of difficulty, so if she were ever to lie down and take up a book, it couldn't be a difficult one.

I'd never read that rubbish, she'd say of this book.

It would give me bad dreams.

At my age, I can't be getting any darker as the lights are soon going out.

Write a nice book, she'll tell you, about nice people, because Bina will warn you raw—you won't find those nice people in the world! You'll have to make them up!

Isn't she gas?

I'm not a gas woman she'd say

And she'd mean it.

She might even repeat it to be sure you heard her.

●

Bina was not a gas woman the first line of my obituary will read.

Don't forget.

Don't forget Eddie left the Tablet on the table when he went. Funnily, it was the Tall Man who noticed it. Don't forget Eddie took off while I was inside prison that week[19] so I didn't see him leave. Don't forget that only for the Tall Man noticing the Tablet on my table, I'd never have known why I was receiving the plethora of abusive messages each time the phone rang. Don't forget, only for these abusive messages down the years I would never have bought an answering machine. If I hadn't bought the answering machine, things would have turned out very different. I'm not saying the answering machine is the reason I was sent down for a week. But the shouty messages on it had nothing got to do with what the papers said about

---

[19] He must have run out the door in a hurry—he left a washing-up bowl and a dog lead in the middle of the kitchen floor. There was crusty egg swimming in my sink.

me. No, as it turned out they were nothing got to do with me at all, they were everything to do with what Eddie was writing on the Tablet.

Don't forget whatever it was that led you to forgetting. Pay attention to the first gesture. See where it starts. For it all goes badly wrong from there. I knew the Tall Man was useful because he kept pointing out small details to me. Do you see that? Do you notice this? God is in the details. There are the useful people and the timewasters. He was also very useful because he was a maniac for Scrabble and I became much stronger at the game. Even though he said there were tiles missing from my box. We'll play on, he said. I enjoy the challenge. He was a good man the Tall Man. At least I thought he was a good man. And where is he now? And what have they done with him, you'll ask. You may very well ask that. Follow the trail. Follow the trail I am giving you here. And speculate.

In the Group, we all agreed that God's in the details and that's why we were all to be very, very careful. We were all to be as careful as each other. We were united in this. God is in the details and Be Careful! We all agreed we had to be careful. Collectively careful. No step mis-stooped. What we hadn't factoried in with all these *Be Carefuls* was there might be an indifferent carp amongst us, a toxic implant who was being careful to say *be careful* while only waiting to spy, witness and snitch what we were all being careful about.

Keep a close eye on what is in people's bags, the Tall Man told me. You're looking for clues to their persuasion. What kind of clues are you looking for, he asked me. Floral tissues, I replied. No ordinary woman who wasn't prying would buy such mad tissues, would she? He looked blank. I don't know about that, he said, but keep your eyes peeled. When you do a home visit, look around the place carefully, note any disadvantages of the layout, be vocally non-committal but assess, he said. Assess, I repeated. I was keen the Tall Man think me capable and not notice that I sometimes forget things. So I made a habit of repeating things after he'd spoken them, like we were in an army arrangement and I was only taking orders from above.

What about the men, he said. You think only women are the spies? He was always after me for the minutiae. Unfortunately, I was not the woman to provide it given my failures with this very slippery gender.

Ask questions, he said. Find out about the family. Find out their views on other things and join the dots. In every question you are gathering evidence of who might be around you and you must take care not to give any information away.

We are taught this.

The Tall Man taught us.

Careful

Careful

Careful

Careful on the details.

Let no detail be spoiled
Extracted
Or uttered
Where it does not belong.

✉

████████ from the Group phoned.
Have you got the hairnets? he asked.
Let there be no panic, I replied.
We can't find them.
We think you have them.
Let there be no panic about hairnets, I repeated.

I wondered if Phil was onto me.
I wondered about what Phil knew.
I did.
Let there be no wondering about that.

✉

████████ from the Group phoned.
Have you got the shoe-cover yokes? she asked.
I let that one fade into the answering machine.

I suspect the Group has been infiltrated
No one ever phoned me this often
Before I was arrested
When I was some actual use to the people who needed me.

Phil was wrong
She didn't need to go.
She could have stuck around.
I was on my way over to tell her that
When she decided she'd had enough[20]
That's what they don't know
The daughters don't know that.
Her angry daughters didn't know their mam at all.
I knew her.
I knew she was wrong.
Oh Phil could be wrong.
Phil was very wrong.
You know.

She misunderstood what I was doing
How I was helping people

---

[20] They accused me of burning her. I did no such thing. I don't even like lighting the cooker.

Who I was helping
Phil took the wrong clues from it.

Do not borrow a handkerchief.

It's a filthy habit.

It has no relevance to anything discussed here, but I just wanted to pass it along as a warning in its own right when watching men. If you spill something and a man offers you his hanky to wipe it up . . . DON'T TOUCH IT AND DON'T GO NEAR IT AND DON'T COME AND TELL ME ABOUT IT AFTERWARDS. Pretend you didn't see it or hear his offer and carry on with your fixing.

Take no help from any man waving or offering a hanky. Maybe take no help from any man waving or offering any-thing, unless he's an ambulance man or selling you a ham. Follow the parade of these warnings, even the random ones I'm hurling in, and they'll be useful. Have no doubt.

I've made all these mistakes for you.

Except the handkerchief one.

I saw a man do that

And it turned my stomach.

The man was Eddie.

The circumstances of the borrow are gone.

But they'll come again.

That's what the doctor said when he interviewed me that time. And if they don't come again I am not allowed to get upset about it. You remember even less when you're upset, Bina, he said.[21]

Don't forget, when you can't remember, it'll come back to you. It'll come again. It can make you ever so panicky, but hold your panic in. Let the old head work its way through it. Let it work its way out through your head. Then you'll remember.

I panicked too much.
It's been a lifetime of panic.
Eddie would make you panic
It's how he is.
Sirenic.
Claxonic.
Awful.
Awful.
Awful.

_____

[21] That doctor will probably testify against me too. They'll be after him I'm sure.

A funny thing is I never panicked at all in prison. I got there on a Tuesday and I was released the Tuesday week. I slept a great deal and I had a few chats.

I wasn't afraid.

Honestly, the only place I've been afraid is inside my own home.

There was even a day inside in the prison where I thought it wouldn't be so bad if I'd to live in there for three or seven years. They keep you busy and they keep you fed.

But it was only one day I thought that way.

And that day was a Wednesday.

And as I've already explained, Wednesday has often been a dangerous day for me.

So the pattern was set and followed me there inside.

A lovely young one came into me one day out of the seven I was in prison.

Was I on drink or drugs or hearing voices?

I wasn't, I said.

Was I sad or miserable?

I wasn't. Not a bit. I was only sorry about the woman who changed her mind—or the daughter who believed she had, for I knew Phil was sure of what she was doing and on account of *that* I wasn't sleeping.

She took my blood pressure and said something was wrong

with me. I asked was she a Muslim and she agreed she was, so I told her about Phil's son Jimmy dying and how Phil and I went to Shannon to protest that time and that Phil liked all the Muslims. She was mad for the Muslims, I said. She made us all go protesting.

That's sad about Jimmy, the lovely one said. And how is your friend now?

She's dead now, I said. She's very dead.

Lift up your vest, I want to listen to your chest, she said.

Deep breath. She put that thing on me and it felt like someone was tapping at me with the back of a big spoon. Deep breath, she kept saying, and all night long I heard her voice saying deep breath, but I paid no heed to it. And now that I think on it that might have been the very first time I had the David Bowie dreams. Ah no. Wait now. It has come back to me. I have it all wrong. I'd had the David Bowie dreams before. That night was not the first time. I'm cross now. This is what is awful annoying about age, the way you can think something is brand new and all strange, when it's nothing of the sort. He was half orange in that first dream. Half his face was the shade of an electric-bar fire. I think I saw him injured in that dream. He wasn't singing, that much I am certain. I knew there was a good reason why Eddie left the Tablet on the table when he fled. I am going to open up the videos and find the faces David Bowie was wearing in every single dream I've had of him.

Since then though, when he speaks to me, Mr. Bowie has that soft, posh London voice. He is like one of those hypnotists talking me down. He's never done telling me to be shut of Eddie. Get rid of him Bina, Bowie says. Kick him out. Reclaim your home! He's not worth it. He's up to no good, he'll say before launching into Golden Ears or whatever song it is he is practising. I sometimes answer him back. Oh Mr. Bowie, if you only knew! I do try to keep it light between us though. He's a pest, I'll say of Eddie, since I wouldn't want David Bowie to know how much I loathe Eddie or he'd stop appearing. It'd turn him off. When you tell men how you actually feel about one of them they don't like it. They don't like it at all. Even David Bowie wouldn't be able for the truth and he's a strong man now. We've always to be jollier than them or they'll turn on you and call you bitter and a miser. Find me the woman in Dickens who is allowed to be utterly miserable. Find me her now while I put the kettle on.

It's a funny thing when the papers write about you or the TV tells about you, but they have not talked to you. They have to imagine your voice. (You won't have to imagine my voice.) They give you a voice based on what they believe your actions are. They talk about you like they are speculating through binoculars: *See that hen in the yard, she looks unwell, she looks unhappy, the hen is wandering about out there burdened with the kinds of questions we have come to expect hens to be burdened with, Yes Jeremy we can confirm at this hour she's a hen. We have confirmed she is wandering about and has a lot of feathers. She might lay an egg. Hens are known to lay eggs but the question of when this decision could be taken is something we don't yet know.* They give you a head and a body. Not your own. They create the sound of your feet and the ticking of your brain. I expect they are generally very good at it, but there's the odd exception and I am and was that exception. I couldn't recognize myself at all, but I was glad they used that old photo of me taking a hammer to the plane that time during the protest at Shannon Airport because I had a hat on.[22]

I was satisfied because I had the warm memory of what drove me to do it and the sheer rising pleasure I experienced during the act. Not unlike the people leaving angry messages on the answering machine having nothing got to do with me, the reason I attacked the plane was nothing to do with politics or protest or war at all, it had everything to do with Eddie.

I was so fed up of him.

We didn't know you were going to do that, the other women said once I'd been hauled off to the police station.

Sure I didn't know myself, I told them.

You never told us, they said.

I didn't know myself, I repeated.

But God was I proud.

It was worth it.

Even how it has come back to double punish me now.

Still worth it.[23]

---

[22] I don't like any photo that has my ears in it.

[23] Always create a spectacle—it can be a very useful thing. Better still have someone else create it and stand there and watch with your arms crossed.

I was mad for a day trip that time,[24] so when the others said they were going on a protest I tagged along. I swear I'd no clue what we were going protesting about. Some vague curry of planes, Iraq, Shannon, bullets in bags and bags inside planes that should not be flying over us. Truly, I didn't care.

On the way there we were given all kinds of instructing on putting fabric over our faces in case of tear gas and make sure you go to the toilet before we begin to climb over or through the fence. There were also people selected to carry the tools and conceal them, those who hadn't been on the protest before. I was honestly just a Sherpa. I wasn't supposed to do anything, except carry the tool, but I got a cheeky feeling I sprung to, which honestly was as surprising to myself as to the people around me. What are you doing, they hissed. And the Gardai who hauled me away asked the same. It was a bit like being in a James Bond film. I've not seen many of them, as they are very noisy and I don't like the sight of himself shirtless, rolling about in bed. Once it all started it was great altogether! I couldn't believe the fun in it. I'd always thought protests were full of griping farmers who should stay home and get a haircut. More and more my indignant feelings about Eddie rose and as we cut the wire fence and crawled through I had the widest sense that I was escaping from Eddie. And, I'll be honest, it was then I went a bit far. I went a bit further than I intended. I went mad!

Some of the things that have been written and said about me are patently untrue. But that day I confess I went a bit far and surprised even myself.

---

[24] See, *Malarky: A Novel in Episodes.*

As I pounded the plane with the hammer, I imagined I was knocking out every one of Eddie's teeth and finally shutting him up. The Guard, Harry, said that time in court that it was very hard to drag me away from the plane and it took four of them to restrain me. ("She was like a mad boar Your Honour and her wild teeth were clenched.")

Of course they were exaggerating.

Of course I didn't tell them about Eddie.

Of course this partly explains why the Crusties are back outside my back door camping and determined to defend me.

You stood up for innocents!

Now we'll stand up for you.

Oh God

Please don't.

Everyone just lie down and have a nap.

A never-ending one.

Jealousy was a factor.

Mr. David Bowie has warned me about it. Yeah Bina, there's a lot of jealousy. And now the pair of us are here warning you.

A crowd of seven sleep-deprived beards and tattoos had gathered outside the Garda station chanting for my release, and when I finally left a rowdy cheer arose like I was a footballer who'd scored a goal. To be honest now I didn't dislike the clapping and cheering, but when they called Speech!

Speech! I demurred and asked for a cup of tea and a piece of toast. I feel like I've had an operation, I said to the two strange young beards hugging me. (The one on the left could have used a good scrub to the armpit region. The one on the right was shouting in my ear, so I couldn't establish what condition of hygiene he was in at all.)

It was a cup of tea I wouldn't forget the taste of in a hurry.

One of them, a Donal, drove me all the way home in his bumpy van, which was full of flags, gas masks and lidded buckets I worried might have urine in them, and three dogs asleep with their legs stretched out. He even had a few traffic cones back there. I fell asleep listening to him gabbling on about Venezuela. He could have murdered me but he didn't.

That fella, the Donal, is not camping outside my back door with the current band of Crusties. I've been told he has a broken leg due to an altercation involving a lamp post near the American embassy. I said outright there's to be no one injured or living on crutches in this encampment. It's an awful shame about the leg as he's likely the only one among them I'd let in for tea or to use my toilet.

Don't forget.

Eddie being Eddie left the evidence flat square with the battery drained out of it in the middle of my kitchen table. Honestly I would have discarded it without a thought. Only that the Tall Man saw it when he snuck in for a final sly visit[25] & Scrabble game we'd grown accustomed to having if he is in the area for the reason he comes to this area and it is a reason I cannot state here.

But you have a Tablet, he said. I thought you couldn't receive emails.

I can't, I said.

You can, he said, and he lifted it up and turned it over.

I can?

And then I could.

Don't forget.

This is how I saw the messages. This is how I saw all the messages Eddie had been posting on the internets. This was the reason for all these people shouting at me down the phone. They were nothing got to do with the Group at all. They weren't angry at me for helping the people I've helped. It was nothing to do with the week I spent in prison. Or the papers calling me a terminally mad woman with a syringe and a bucket. They were angry at Eddie. And because Eddie put my phone number up there on the internets, they became angry at me. He wrote *my* phone number under his name where he shouted at people on the Tablet. The Tall Man showed me the messages, or postings, as he called them. *Beefcake Eddie*, Eddie had named himself, and he had put a picture of the Incredible Hulk wearing a party hat and had

---

[25] The Tall Man paid me one final visit wearing the missing shoe coverings to give over his final instructions.

described himself as *Pizza, Single With a Septic Tank & ready to take your call right now. What are ye waitin fer . . . form an orderly queue laydies . . . 096* ▬▬▬▬

What is it? Has he us advertised for pizza? Is that why there are so many angry calls?

The Tall Man fiddled a bit with the tip of his finger and pinched at the screen and up the postings flashed. I couldn't read them. Too small. So out he called them to me. He was neither happy nor unhappy as he read them and only at one point did he remind me that it wasn't necessary for me to know the details of them. You have a fulfilling life Bina,[26] he said, and listening to this man's ravings will not enhance it. It is of no benefit for you to hear this.

Read on, I commanded him.

"I KNEW OF A WOMAN ON THE WESTPORT TRAIN LAYERS OF CLOTHING. HIDING A BOMB INSIDE A FROZEN CHICKEN. !!!! HATE FUCKIN WESTPORT."

"GET RID OF THE SCARF HEADS SEND THEM BACK TO THE DESERT WITH THEIR CAMELS."

"ISIS LIVING IT UP IN FOXFORD. BUS DRIVER IS A GAY ISIS MAGGOT. BEHEAD HIM. SEND HIS HEAD BACK TO ALEPPO."

---

[26] He was a great man for conveniently failing to notice I could be heading to prison for 15 years imminently.

(There were an awful lot of messages about a particular bus driver in Foxford who Eddie insisted stole his tool bag. I can't recall Eddie owning any such tool bag.)

"MAN WITH BEARD WORKING AT CENTRA DELI IS A PEDO. DO NOT BUY FOOD THERE. SPAYCIALLY THE HAM. HAM IS CONTAMNATED."

"WHY ARE YOU HERE? GO AWAY. GO BACK. ISRAEL BUILD A WALL. COME BUILD A WALL. WALL IN THE CENTRA YOU KNOW WHERE TO FIND THE ISIS COCK SUCKER. HE IS WORKING IN THE DELI AND NAME IS MICHAEL. WEARING A BADGE WITH MICHAEL ON IT."

And on and on he'd tiraded about Westport. That Westport was full of terrorists. That beheadings were happening on the train. In the toilet. That there was frozen chicken that was full of bombs. That. That. That.

I was exhausted.

Come again? I said. He's out of his mind. I only ever took a felting course in Westport. I bought a few jars of honey and I ate a bowl of soup. I don't know if he's ever even been to Westport in all the years I was lumbered with him. What has he agin Westport? He's gone out of his mind.

He is and he has, the Tall Man said, and shook up the bag of Scrabble tiles to remind us more serious business awaited. I haven't long, he said watching the kitchen window.

As the Tall Man read onward, the themes of Eddie's announcements changed into football, Arsenal giving away goals and THIS GOVERNMENT and the Tall Man explained

Eddie never stopped going on about THIS GOVERNMENT and he was very angry about the Arsenal Manager until his regalings were terminated on the date I estimate he fled from here. In particular, Eddie fixated viciously on certain politicians and individual footballers and then more pedestrian topics were dipped into: a complaint about a broken lamp, an inquiry as to whether fishing licences were yet in stock. Finally he seemed to settle down and talked mostly of women who'd been murdered or tragically killed in accidents—like he cared—and then he screamed about football matches in between his THIS GOVERNMENT ARE ALL PEDOS GIVING EVERYTHING TO PEDO JUDGES in CAPITAL LETTER BROADCASTS.

How do I get my telephone number off there?

The Tall Man said he had no idea how it could be done. It was hard to have anything taken off the internets and that was why it was important not to let anything get onto it. You need to think of it as a tunnel, he said. You pass through it, you don't dawdle examining the tiles or someone might clunk you over the head with the butt of a rifle. Brisk and briskly, he said. No lingering.

I hadn't a clue what he was talking about, but being tired and inclined to mental weariness I didn't concern myself any further over his cluttery meanings.

Don't forget

This was the difference between myself and the Tall Man, he was always on edge, kept moving and on his guard. I wasn't. I didn't really give too much bother because I was only ever trying to get away from Eddie for a few hours. The Tall Man had me warned.

Sometimes he even wore a disguise like he was a minister. Once he wore long robes like a monk. He looked very strange. Uniforms are good, the Tall Man said. No one looks twice at anyone wearing a uniform. I confess I looked three times at him as the robe was tied funny and a bit small on him.

When I thought back through the telephone messages I now understood why people were offering to kill and torture me or were chiding me over my disgusting hatred and attitudes to the Arabians. There was only one poor simpleton asking to add extra pineapple to his previous order. And when I went back to find his first order he had phoned three times to tell me extra cheese and no healthy crust and could I cut one slice of pizza into small chunks because his father struggled with his teeth.

It also explained the drunk giggler calling herself Fatima and saying into my phone in a horsey snort, *come and get me bhoy*. And ringing back to *see if I hadn't noticed the first time, she was in the queue* and a third time, the next morning, to apologize and ask that I erase the message and that I should never ever phone the number she'd given because her husband would murder the pair of us. *I was drunk and I am regretful and my name is not Fatima so do not look for me*, she said into my answering machine, which I found both terribly honest and formal.

And how did you never figure these messages were strange, the Tall Man wanted to know. To be honest now after the first few I stopped pressing the button and just let them mount up. Anyone who was looking for me knew well where to find me here behind my back door, and anyone I wanted to speak to wouldn't phone me this way to begin with. They'd never leave a message, and you could say I severed from my phone. It sounds worse than it is. I was so delighted Eddie was gone, but more worried about lifting the phone and finding him there than never speaking to another soul again.

Another warning just slipped in there.

Watch your phone.

Watch who has your number and who gives out your number.

Never write it on your phone.

Keep it private.

Keep it off the internets.

Don't listen to the answering machine. Don't even have one. Anyone who wants you will know where to find you. Behind your door. Tell them to text. Only do texting. You can delete texting. You can ignore text. You can silence text. It's hard to erase those lunatics bellowing out of your answering machine, even if they are funny, which they sometimes are.

It took a Tablet I didn't know I had and a stranger to disclose the simple facts of the matter. As it is. As it always is. If you are looking at a person it's hard to say the things you might whisper very comfortably behind a pillow or a curtain. The here and the there. And don't mind the ones who'll say it's neither here nor there. It's absolutely both here and there. I'm here and he's there and finally I can say what should have been said from here to there. And that was most certainly a warning.

No *ah well, toss it off.*

Toss it on.

Pile it on.

Tell it all.

Once you're in the protected shadow of an exit.

A short inventory will now take place:

I let

1. Eddie in
2. The Tall Man in

I was let in by

Tomás

Phil

Others I cannot name here.

I place this inventory here as evidence. Why did she let him in, you are probably asking, as indeed I am, but if you look at the total number of people who let me in you can see that it's not unreasonable to let people in. It's what we do. We let people in. How it is.

The trouble lies in getting them back out.

Let that sink in or register before you open your door and say the fateful words *come in* or worse still, *would you like a cup of tea?*

Imagine instead there's no tea where you live and where there's none, there's none worth offering.

Are we agreed?

Grand so, we'll go on.

Tomás is why.

Why we make the videos.

I'd have been in prison if we didn't have his video

I might still be yet

Because Phil didn't make a video

Her daughters are after my gullet.

Daughters who never visited her when she was alive

Want to bring her back

To not visit her

All over again.

They love revising the dead over the living

No one has any time for you until you're dead.

And undemanding.

Then there's nothing they won't do for ye.

How it is.

Once you're dead

Everyone loves you

Once you're dead.

Everyone's defending you

Once you're dead.

Hurry up and be dead if you want to be liked.

The Tall Man is usually gone after the video.

He records it and departs.

Totes and uploads it.

It's explained to the departee.

Long, hard, syllabled out to them.

If you ingest

You will divest.

If this pill goes down the hatch, you'll fear no more the heat of the sun. There will never be any sun again. Latch closed. Lights out. Dead as a duck. Well, my ducks.

Of course they know.

How would you ask for that pill and believe it's a vitamin as Phil's daughters are claiming.

And

Believe you me when I tell you it takes some serious amount of asking before you'd get it.

Eddie hit me on the head.

I was very surprised.

He hit me on the head awful suddenly

And he didn't notice doing it.

He just carried on and asked was there orange juice in the fridge.

It was incidental, as if he'd ticked off something on a list or scratched the ears on a cat.

I would like to say that it was after he hit me on the head I started forgetting things. Like the bank card I have mentioned or I am going to mention because I can't recall everything I mention as I am mentioning it, but that would likely be a lie. I am trying to practise not lying for the court appearance. I am trying to practise direct, bold honesty, no matter the consequences.

Because for years,

I did no such thing.

The doctor asked me about the bruise on my neck.

Did you fall?

I did.

Did you fall onto something?

I came here to get a urine test, I said, not the Spanish Inquisition.

I want to listen to your chest, he said.

You'll do no such thing. I never heard of chests being listened to when it's my kidney that's complaining.

But he insisted.

And I complied.

Because I thought he'd report me or write a report on me as the whole world, it seems, is being paid to write reports on me, which is another good reason why I am writing my own report (on me) right here for you.

Are you afraid of anyone? Is anyone stealing from you? he asked.

Do I look afraid of anyone?

He put the stethoscope around his neck and asked me to look left and right.

He checked the back of my ears and I winced because my ear was still painful back where Eddie had thumped me. He stared at my forearms and turned over my two palms.

You can get dressed, he said.

When he handed me the antibiotic, he instructed me to come back and see him again next week.

I'll tell you the truth. I never went near him again.

He was too good a doctor and I'd be in too much trouble if he sent someone to the house to see why was I bruised.

I needed another solution

This much I knew.

That's another warning.
If you know you need another solution
Don't dilly dawdle on it.
Or you'll only attract suspicion.
If you're going to attract suspicion
Save yourself the bother
Just divulge the truth to someone you trust
Tell them to deliver the information to the world on your behalf.
Once you're dead.
Whisper it
Write it
However it might be imparted
Just somehow let it be said.

Don't leave people wondering
The way Phil has me left wondering.
It creates a whole new round of inexplicable brokenness and bruises
Only these ones are worse because they're
Unseen.
Only you can feel them
In spaces you didn't think could be broke.
Trust me when I tell you
All of it and all of you can be even more broke
Than you can see or imagine.

Make a pact.
I don't know how
But make pacts
With those who are worrying you.

Once I tried to make one with a man who worried me.
A simple pact that he'd go to the doctor.
Will you promise me you'll go to the doctor on Monday,
I said.
I can't promise you that, he said.
And I remembered that too-good doctor and
I knew well the man who wouldn't promise me didn't
want to be saved
Which was why when the Tall Man came
I helped.
I did it without a second thought.
I did it for those who don't want saving.
Rather than punish them
For knowing it.
And leaving them with it.
And leaving it with them.
For I know what it is to be trapped
Because I was trapped.
I trapped myself.

I know all this and no one needs to tell me it.
I am 74 years old and I know a lot of things.

And these poor blighters who didn't want to be saved
hadn't trapped themselves
Instead
Their bodies had bolted on them.
Or bolted them inside their houses.
In a manner that you can't negotiate a way around.
Only declare a way out.
An exit.

So
Instead
Therefore
Better you assume if you are stupid enough to let a man
like Eddie into your kitchen, he's very likely to hit you on
the head.

I tried to tackle him: You hit me on the head.
I did not.
You did.
When?
Yesterday.
I don't remember that.
I showed him the cut and bruise over my ear.

Really, he said. Are you sure?

He spat a bit onto his hand and rubbed his palm up against it.

It was one of the kinder things he did.

He left his cupped palm up against it for a few seconds in penance.

If you ever do it again, I said, I'll have you shot.

He never hit me on the head again.

But the words I issued were unfortunate.

These are the words he's given over to the authorities now.

See how he can take the sheet from under me.

Even from afar.

Because I wouldn't give him the land, see.

(He was at me to sign it over to him)

I'm stupid but not that stupid.

I see them coming once they are here.

Like icebergs, I suppose.

When they are on top of you

You feel them.

You say, ah there you are.

I see you because I can feel you.

Then you drown.

But when someone hits you on the head you feel it and you see them.

Incontrovertible
Intractable.
Scrabble has all the words for it.
Once you know your letters
You find all the words
That score.
Careful with the language lads.
Watch the language there.
Pay attention to the letters.
That was obviously a warning.
It'll come back for you.

I play Scrabble for this reason. As a reminder. To remind myself what all the combining of letters and words can achieve and to keep myself in check. If I play it here, I have no further need to play in life. There should be no more surprises at my age other than upon the Scrabble board.

Are we agreed?
We're not.
Right.
On we go.

There were a lot of disagreements in the Group. Often the disagreements were nothing to do with the Group at all. They were disagreements over maps and directions and who told who and what time and I don't like the way that fella says and she's a bit cold and minor stuff that could become medium stuff without you even noticing.

I kept one of the plastic bags. The Exit bags. Or Hoover bags as we called them on the phone. I kept one for myself and I think that's why the Group keep phoning. They probably want that bag for someone else. They might think with all the trouble I've caused I don't deserve a bag. I don't agree with them. But if they come here and ask me for it I'll hand it over. I'm just not for doing deliveries these days. I'm in bed, where I'm staying warm and waiting for whatever the verdict is.

Isn't it funny that never happens in reverse? That the major stuff like a big lump of Eddie doesn't become minor or medium stuff without you noticing? The major stuff only becomes minor stuff if you disappear on it entirely. Or I suppose if you are lucky enough, in the rare case, to have it disappear on you. Or have someone else disappear it for you.

That seems to happen a lot in hotels and at boxing matches these days. And it's nasty men is doing it. I am not in hotels or at boxing matches and I wouldn't give money to a nasty man to solve my problems. I'm in bed so I suppose nothing is going to change that way for me. Not even my sheets, unless I get up and change them.

I believe in merciful releases. I do. More people should pray for them. Even if it involves asteroids.

The smell you create is the smell that follows you into the ground, as my mother, God rest her, would say.

In the ground now

Never left a smell

She.

She wouldn't be happy about these sheets. *The Lord save us Bina, would you get up and move about, never mind lying there like a stuffed pig. There's work to be done and nothing gets done only by looking at it. If you see it needing doing, get on with it*, she'd say. *If it smells, wash it! If it doesn't need saying, shut up and leave it unsaid!*

Listen to mothers, they know a lot about smells.

What they mean and how to locate them.

Eddie was clueless about smells

He smothered the place with them

And him gone.

And me stuck here still again with all the smells *he* created.

What harm?

Plenty harm is what.

I don't know if I'll convey the scale of (the) harm before the red dot.

My mother wouldn't approve at all of what I am saying here. *How many times have I told you? Too many times to tell you again!* That's what she'd say to all this. When I came back from England a hairy failure she merely said wash your hair, we'll say no more about it, but I knew she was angry. She was angry for years. It's why I stopped still and was in no hurry to make changes. I wanted to be reliable. She didn't mind that since she needed someone to bring her places and drop things off. I became very good at ferrying things about. I was practical in my rehabilitation. I became very good at picking up things I dropped and hiding matters I wanted no person to know about.

Another warning: Careful what you think you are hiding, as it's probably on full view. Careful not to hide suffering because you are only making more work for the people who have yet to discover it. Complain. Complain. Complain. Suffer loud and plentiful or be doomed.

For months afterwards, Eddie asked what did I say before he hit me on the head. And explained that if he couldn't recall striking me whatever I said must have set him off. It was down to the drink. And he was going joining some group 20 miles away for people gone mad on the drink and who were going mad getting off it. He hinted they'd eventually invite me in to be apologized to, because it had happened last week and the invited-in woman had cried and recovered and cried again when she was apologized to by the man who crashed her car, ran over her foot and her cat and more generally destroyed his life, her life and the cat's life. Eddie was keen to tell me she'd cried twice. Like there's salvation in the repetition of suffering.

You were off the drink when you hit me on the head, I wanted to tell him, but I honestly couldn't think of a single good reason for doing so.

Instead I said nothing and I will tell you, sometimes saying nothing can be the most powerful thing with such a man. Because men like Eddie, bullies in woollens, expect you to mend them. They expect you to patch over what they say and what they have done, and in saying nothing, I would be doing no mending. If I'd spoken, he would be easy relieved.

I would warn you not to meet the eyes of a man who is a bully. You cannot negotiate with a bully. You cannot give in to a bully. You can glower. Silence can be surprisingly powerful when it is accompanied by no mending whatsoever.

Remember that.

Turn on your heel.

Walk away.

Or better, when they hello

Don't respond.

Don't make them feel better.

Leave them with what they have achieved.

They work very hard to become the catastrophes they are.

I am not suggesting that getting sent to prison is the only effective action that results in the removal of a snuck-into-your-home man or woman catastrophe, but in my case it did work.

Otherwise Eddie never would have budged.

I had to become worse than who he thought he was himself.

Except, it should be understood, he still has no idea how bad he is.

Has she warned you about Thursdays?
Bina doesn't like Thursdays.
I don't like Tuesdays either, she'll tell you.
Tuesday Wednesday Thursday are the bad days.
Weekly.

Have you got that now?
Is it clear?
Are we clear?
Was that a warning?
She is starting to wonder.
Hard to remember what's gone on above
Without going back.
If it's back Bina goes, she'll lose us.

On.
On.
On I must go
To reach the red dot.

Who are you here for?
Your son is it?
Within is he?
What's that?
Unconscious you say.

Lord save us, did he live?
Not my son
Just that I was the one found him
In the ditch

Beside my wall
Did she say that?

You're a relative is it?
No, no he's the son of a neighbour.
Maeve that's fine
She's fine
She's family
She can come in.
Grand Maeve
No that's fine.
Maeve said Bina could come in.

Hello again.
How are you?
He's in better form today
Not awake yet
But he's showing more signs of life.
It'll be nice there's someone here to welcome him back.
Makes a difference to the recovery when there's family
around.
Big family is it
Brothers has he
Parents.
Dead
We think.
No, I know his uncle, he's not well himself
Is that right.

Awful sad, will anyone come in, we sometimes think.

I often ask myself in this job

Would anyone come?

That.

Do you think everyone asks that?

Oh they do.

They do.

That.

See it

All the time

In here

We wait

To see

Does anyone come?

Sometimes

The odd time

A rare time

They don't.

You could go out of here in a box or even an urn and no one would notice you were gone.

Urns?

Oh yes, urns are all the rage

Like when there's no one like to collect them?

Cheaper

Sssssh.

Wouldn't want that to get out

These days, huh?

Oh yes.

Dreadful lonely.

Where do you send them if

No one?

Rehab

When there's no one at home.

If there's a bed!

Or even no home to go to?

Laughs.

Common these days

Oh it is.

Pushed out I suppose.

Or have *pushed* themselves out

Both.

Cruel though.

It is.

If there's no one to go home to, sometimes they can never go home.

He's young though.

Even the young.

Usually someone comes in for you if you're young.

Hello again.

You're back.

Who are you here for?

Ah he'll be glad

There's been no one

Since

Last you were in.

Did anyone locate the parents or the family?

Ask the social worker.

She'll be down to you now.

●

Bina's stopped saying she's not family anymore.

●

You a relative
You the social worker
Any contact
Can you help?
We were hoping
Have to move him.
Beds are needed.
Patients on trolleys.
Too many trolleys
So many car accidents
You wouldn't believe
Oh I believe
Driving like drunk monkeys the young.
What's his story?
I've no idea
Only he drove into my wall.
Of your house?
Field
And landed in a ditch.
Miracle he wasn't killed.
It is.

Will you find him a place?
Well we'll have to.
A neighbour you say
Can you take him?
Me?
Me take him?
No. No. I can't take him.
They do better with company.
Even temporary.
Well I suppose if it were temporary.
Until he can go to his uncle or wherever he came from
Oh temporary would be a great help.
We'll support you.
And you're family and we prefer family to take them.
Well I am not really close family
Well you know what I mean
More family than he'll have in here or any facility.
Full of old people
Frustrating for the young
And we need the beds for the lesser able
But he's brain injured?
Not at all. No, no. He's just bruised.
He should recover fine.
How long?
A few weeks
Of physio.
I've seen some not make any progress in fifteen years.
He's the lucky one.
Better progress if someone minds them
Always.

Right so.
But just temporary you say
That's it.
We'll send help out to you.
Have you stairs?
I have none.
Great, he wouldn't be able for stairs yet.
There's no stairs.

●

No stairs written down in the paper file.
It was a social worker who wrote it down
Bina wasn't sure would it be taken serious.
Perhaps she felt like she was being selected
Rather than lumped.
Rather than all there was.

●

And with that Eddie was out.

Out into my back bedroom.

You need to act mad, Phil said again.

Go completely mad temporarily. Have a giant conniption, she said. Hurl a pile of cakes or crackers around in Dunnes Stores. Or on the bus.

I never get the bus, I said. Sure, there's no buses. I'd have to go to Dublin to find a bus. Or I'd have to go mad on the bus to Dublin and everyone would ignore me because they have the headsets on them.

Don't go too mad is all, Phil said, or you'll end up dragged off the bus in Roscommon, or worse, Longford. That's no place for a woman to be alone and mad. You'd be better off in Limerick, where the hospitals are warmer. If you do it properly then they'll stick you someplace warm. Then you'll be shut of him. Because as soon as you're mad he'll leave. It's always the way. They drive you mad and then they leave. They drive you mad to be shut of you, so get going first yourself.

Oh I said he has me driven mad. He absolutely has.

I'm telling you, Phil said. You've to make him afraid of you, if you ever want to be shut of him. You've to figure out, briefly, how to be more terrifying than he is. You won't have to do it for long and it'll work.

Get sick, Phil said. If you are sick like me then he'll have to go.

I'm not sick, I said. The only sick I am is sick of Eddie and I invited that sickness upon myself. It's as if I stuck my head in a freezer full of smallpox.

Phil grimaced.

Don't, she said

That is a terrible image. It'll give me bad dreams.

I was tempted to tell Phil about the David Bowie dreams but I did not. I wasn't sure what way she felt about him and whether she might think me cracked.

Phil said she had read a book on death dreams and that if you were having them it meant your time was up.

I don't know about that, I said.

Have you had any dreams of killing Eddie, she asked.

Oh, I said. I have. Non-stop from the day his head hit the pillow.

●

Phil asked Bina to do things
They were difficult things
The things that Phil asked her to do.

Never been an easy woman Phil.
Since Jimmy died[27] she'd lapsed dreadful
But she wasn't ever as difficult as this.
The way she was about this particular thing
The thing she wanted Bina to do.
A thing that was technically wrong for Bina to do.

●

---

[27] See, *Malarky: A Novel in Episodes.*

But you've done it before, Phil said to me.
You don't know that though. Me, warily, back.
You have and you will again, came she.

I may have and then again, I may not have.
We went on like this like two cats.
Back and forth a volley of vagueness
Kindly but vaguely.

You're going no place
I said to her
You're going no place that I'm not going.
Well.
She said.
Just that.
Well.
Open-ended well for me to fall into.
Come with me.

Think on this.

I'm warning you that people might and do ask you to do difficult things.

You might persuade yourself they are easy things when asked.

They might become less easy once they are done.

Be careful now about what a person might ask you to do.

That's all this here warning can be.

More hint than warning.

It was very difficult when Phil started asking me to help her. I never should have told her what I was doing, but I was an awful woman for starting a sentence before I'd thought through where it might lead me. I was in a tunnel before I realized I couldn't find a clear way around it. You only have backwards or forwards in a tunnel.

I did put the idea inside her head
By confiding to her what I had done

Once.

Only once, mind.

At least I only told her about that one.

The one that was Tomás.

Tomás remained with me, where the others have fled.

It's how it is.

Or was.

Nothing you can do about it

Nothing you can do with it.

Except continue to tell the woman no,

Put a sock in it.

Whisht, would ya

I will not do the difficult thing you ask.

Hard to say no though, when they are looking at you

And they're asking you.

You try it

Say no.

Say no to your mother or someone

You're taught never to say no to.

Then come back to me.

I'll do it once you've done it.

I had confided to Phil what I was doing, the thing I cannot
name here for fear I'll put the same idea into your head, the

way I put the idea into her head. I must have said no to her 32 times. It wasn't 32 times nearly enough because she threatened she'd go on her own, if I wasn't going to help.

No. No. No. No. No. No. No. No. No. No. No. No. No. No. No. No. No. No. No. No. No. No. No. No. No. No. No. No. No. No. No. No.

This is what no 32 times looks like.

Very good, carry on so.

She asked would I do one thing for her and she'd ask no more than this. What is it? Will you come here and tidy me up before anyone sees me?

She was fixated on being tidy and presentable in her finale. Her anxiety lay in having read, she did not say where, her bowels would empty themselves all over the floor and some-one, a stranger, would find her laid out among them and it would be a terrible sight to inflict on anyone. You know, she said. Your debris is your debris but you must also think of the poor beggar who'll land in on it. They could slip. On account of it being Phil she grew an impish look about her eyes and twitched her nose to the right and said, I'd offer to do the same for you in return only . . .

I agreed swiftly it would be dreadful for someone to come upon you flat dead in a heap of your own shite and I agreed very firmly it was a very good reason not to do it. Not to intentionally put yourself dead into a heap of your own shite.

I never heard a better reason for not doing something, I told her. And clever sneak that she was, she laid that question on me again. Swift.

So you'll do that much for me?

I'll think about it, I said.

Periodically, she pressed me when I visited her. I thought about ceasing my visits. Each time she pressed, I would say only I was still thinking about it.

What way are you leaning, she'd ask.

I'll tell you once I'm leaned.

I did what I could to distract her but when a person's mind is made up, up it is made.

She was clever, mind. She'd tighten me into conversations and I'd be in them and quizzed before knowing they'd even started. And if she caught me withholding, she was savage. It's only the facts I am after, she'd say, and you've given them facts you now deny me to perfect strangers. I'd bet you'd talk about them on the television if they disguised you.

I thought about it while she held my gaze.

I might, I said.

It's different telling a blank nation of strangers things because you can't see them. You can't imagine them walking a life's worth of years in these roads the way I can you. And when you've seen someone in their life, it's hard to concede or sanction them an early exit.

And have you seen me walking about lately? I am barely able to move anymore. Sure what is there for me to walk toward even if I were able?

You've your faith, I said. None of those people I helped had any faith. It was a convenient myth I often deployed to tempt people otherwise in these circumstances. Faith is a mighty weapon to use against the faithful. You can persuade them of all sorts.

I've no faith, Phil said. I only claimed I did to stop people coming over with prayer books. I was worn out with novenas. I said it to have people deliver my shopping. When they think you've faith, they'll do anything. If you act like a heathen they'll behave like heathens. They only want the faithful to carry on and live. If you had a referendum they'd vote to put all the heathens into the fire.

Not anymore, I said. That's all finished in this country.

Well when you are our age, she said, you shouldn't be hanging around in the way. There was a shard of truth in what she said. A woman proud of her home. She swept and mopped that kitchen floor every morning, no matter that there was no one walking on it. I never mopped my floor and I joked with her whether she could skip a day on her own and come over and do mine instead.

No woman should be terrorized inside her home, right?
Agreed.

No woman should be terrorized by her own floor.

I suppose. But she could stop mopping it.

If a woman is terrorized by her floor then should the floor go or should the woman vacate?

Neither.

Why not?

No reason.

Why not?

Woman usurps floor.

Not if the woman can neither put her foot onto her floor in any comfort nor if the floor is coming up to meet her.

I was stumped. She had me.

Physically, Phil had declined. I can't go into too many details because she wouldn't be happy with me. I shouldn't even be using her name here, but they already have her named in the papers.

How is Forty Guts?

How's the enemy?

Phil never called him Eddie.

Leaba

I went to bed.

Three times I went to bed.

Or rather I took to the bed

Three. Separate. Times.

How could you go to bed three times together? That's silly.

When I say I went to bed I don't mean the way you go to bed, the way you probably went to bed last night or the way you might be in bed right now, reading this. I don't mean I go to bed with a person. When I go to bed, I really go to bed. Alone. All alone. There's no one invited in. There's no one to invite in. The first time I went to bed I didn't get back up for two months. This time I haven't counted. But it's probably been more than five days since I lay down and started writing this. I never before wrote anything lying down and that's a fact. I'm not for writing things down but the Tall Man trained me. Have your story straight if questions are asked. You'll only get one go at a reply, he warned me, and he's right.

How'd you, why'd you do it, I hear you ask.

Do you doubt me?

You doubt me?

Never doubt me when it comes to bed.

No woman was ever as good as I am at going to bed.

You'd have to actually be a bed to better me.

Another reason I cannot go to prison. They are fussy about when you go to bed and it won't suit me. I never liked how they make you get out of the bed when they decide you've to be out of it and you've no way out of bed even if you have no desire to be in it.

Desire and decisions, see. A natural contradiction. A place for unnatural eruption.

Eddie was an eruption.

A natural disaster.
The first human one.
Won't be the last.
Plus he's still going
Erupting and disrupting.

Like today
He might be gone
But look at what he left in his wake.

A wake is an absolutely cheery goodbye.
There will be no wake with Eddie.
Except an earthquake.

It'd take an earthquake maybe
To really be shut of him.
Pity you can't order them over the phone, underneath specific people.

She wanted gone from Eddie.
From Eddie, Bina wanted gone.
If she couldn't get rid of him
They could take her.
If it was between the two of them
This weary woman wasn't fussy whom they took.

Phil had suggestions.

Phil said act like she, Bina, was going mad, to get a holiday from Eddie. Then, while inside, send in the heavies to evict him from her house. Bina asked Phil where would she find the heavies and could she find them without going mad? Phil told Bina there were worse things than lying in a white room and having an egg cooked for you. Phil had been in the ward,[28] remember.

Bina remembers. Bina visited her in the ward. She doesn't remember any white room though. With Phil in the ward, all she recalled was the pink bedside cabinet and that whale of a

---

[28] See, *Malarky: A Novel in Episodes.*

lunatic man in the bed opposite, baying non-stop about Beirut and Joanie squawking all manner of unnecessary everything to the nurses.

And the smell.

Oh God the smell.

Or was it multiple smells.

She performed an inventory.

1. The smell of hospital food
2. Or was it sheets
3. Or someone's innards.

She recalled hearing something slop into the bedpan of the woman beside Phil. Another nearby wailed that a tape-worm had eaten its way into her back passage and she bellowed that no one should be lying on these mattresses until they'd been checked for worms.

There would be no holiday from Eddie if there were terrible smells to contend with.

It's true there was likely to be a lingering smell of Eddie in the house.

But whatever the smell once she got rid of him, at least she could breathe.

Could she persuade them she needed taking away from Eddie?

Ideally they'd take Eddie away instead.

This was Bina suggesting to Phil as they discussed it.

They don't take you unless you're dying now.

This was Phil suggesting to Bina as they discussed it.

Dead.

You've to be dead.

Or mad.

If you're mad enough they'll take you.

Phil said.

That was Phil.

That had her thinking.

Phil had that effect. She was one of the very few who did this to Bina.

All this was of course

During Eddie

Eddie wasn't gone, the way he is now.

Now she doesn't struggle with how to get away from him

She just worries he'll come back.

●

I went to bed to think about Phil's suggestions.

I did not get up for two months.

Basically.

But I might have to scrub this out.

I might not want the exact amount of time to be known.

Would you think a woman lazy who'd done that (just taken to the bed) or would you think her sane? Some might think she/I was just a lazy woman.

I am not a lazy woman. I promise you that. Should I tell you what I did to survive Eddie or should I keep that quiet? These are decisions I must make if I am to give you the warnings.

Will it look bad in the court if I admit I went to bed? Or will it seem much less likely I was running around killing people as they are claiming it.

●

Bina remembers no one listens to her.
Not Eddie
Not Phil
Not the Tall Man
No one.

●

How about: I was a woman wrestling deep struggle and contemplation and it was only the scale of the blight of Eddie, and my inability to successfully remove him that laid me down flat.

Or is it better to have the flat truth flattened: How could I, a woman as robust and cautious as I am, not just have placed myself in, but have actively sustained, this predicament? It would all cause you pause. It would cause you all pause. And let's face it if I pause I will never reach the red dot. And nor will you.

It's a lot of work, thinking.
People don't realize how much work it is.
Even if you're lying down.
It's not easy to tame time or tether the glorious mind.

Of course, you do a bit of scheming if you're heading to bed long-term. You don't just hop in. You need a few basics if you are planning on not moving. These are the things I would warn you to organize before you get into the bed.

1. Kettle
2. Bucket
3. Tea
4. Biscuits
5. Books, knitting, tasks
6. Electric blanket
7. Clean vests.
8. Mouthwash
9. Small plastic container
10. Any medicine you take daily
11. Phone with long extension to pass under the door
12. Big stick in case of intruders
13. Whistle in case stick doesn't deter
14. Sweets
15. Tight stockings for your varicose veins
16. Radio
17. Torch as light and weapon
18. Knife in case big stick, whistle & torch fail you
19. Paracetamol
20. Ginger cake (unlikely to be stolen, it's an acquired taste & doesn't mould quick)

I could have planned it better, but all in all I did well. Like I said, I am very good at going to bed. When I've had enough, my mind shuts and into the bed I take myself.

This is the most frightening state a woman can enter because if you are in bed you are suddenly no use to anybody and it's only then they realize how much use you were. If I were to warn you in relation to going to bed, I would only advise not to wait too long to do so, but hold out as long as you can once supine. Do not budge or they won't take you serious. And you won't take yourself serious either.

●

An agreement was reached.
An agreement was reached between the two women.
The way women agree to such things.

●

Phil & I had agreed to it the way we have agreed to things for the lifetime we have known each other. We agree this way. One or the other of us says something and the other doesn't disagree. That's all it takes. We knew we'd agreed because when she'd asked me, every other single time, whether I would do what she wants me to do, I had a reply for her and she, in turn, had an answer for me. I said only I'd think about it, fully intending never to think about it. This time my response was different. My response was a quietly considered but firm *grand*. She was probably taken aback because, although she knew agreement might one day come, she probably had not expected it that soon. I had not known that all agreement would require was for me to lie down. Once I lay down in my bed, Phil's reasoning about her exit made absolute sense.

You've to understand I am not warning you not to lie down or to reach this conclusion faster. If anything, anytime I've lain down it has been a great deal more fruitful than whenever I've stood up. Generally, as long as you put a bit of planning into it and bar the door, the bed is about the only place you can be guaranteed peace. No sooner have you peace do you see what needs to be done. And what did I see? I'll tell you what I saw. I saw my own bed empty and I saw Phil's bed needing emptying. It flushed over me: it was time for me to be gone and her to be gone because if I were gone, or to go first, she'd have no one who'd be anywhere near being able to get her gone, only herself. And this had long been her contention, that had she the means she'd already be gone and I was doing no justice to either of us by holding her up.

I failed to see her logic when she pinned it me this way. I couldn't even see the border of her wallpapered reasoning. I thought she was clean crackers, which was a local murmured rumour I personally paid no heed to. There's nothing the matter with that woman, I told them that time at the hospital. And hasn't she levelled that back to me bang, bang, boomerang between my eyes? You, she said into the phone in my ear— for when I took to the bed we sometimes held thrice daily conversations—sure it was you warned me not to let them put anything in my mouth nor up the other end either, and if they had done, maybe now I wouldn't be stuck marooned, maybe they would have finished me off.

Ah that was different.

How was it different?

They were against you then.

And it's you who are against me now?

I'm not a bit against you, I said. I'm for you. I'm all for you sticking around.

Who's going to wipe my arse when I can't reach it? Will you wipe it?

I will.

And how will you wipe it laid up there in your bed?

I'll get out of my bed.

Get out of your bed now.

I'm not ready to get out of my bed.

I was stubborn on this point, as I'd only just gotten into my bed.

And Phil resorted to they'd given her three months to live and I resorted to they'd given her anywhere from three months to three years and we both resorted to silence. The kind of silence that drips, where all that needed to be said was being thought and we would never get beyond these thoughts without one or the other of us protesting.

We're no good to one another in these states, Phil said to me another time on the phone.

We're grand, I said. There's worse than us.

She didn't believe me. And I didn't believe me. But we moved on from the big old fencepost staking the truth and the two of us apart.

Has Forty Guts gone? Phil said.

He has in his arse.

I know how you can get him gone, she said as she sat in her chair looking weaker than I'd ever seen her. Her right hand was failing her. It's like a claw, she said, and what use have I for a claw.

It's true I went to bed that first time to think, but quite honestly, I also took to the bed for safety.

Out of nowhere, Eddie started physically hitting/shoving/waving his hands close to my face. The threat of a hit, the start of a hit becoming a shove, a push and a bump or jostle. And the only place I felt safe was in bed. It's very hard to hit someone if they are inside their bedroom lying flat with the door locked. See, he'd hit me in sly ways and only in the kitchen or if I'd cause to hand him a cup. I kept forgetting this. Give me that cup he'd say and I'd reach for the cup and he'd strike me every time. He would slam the bottom of his hand under the cup if there was hot liquid in it and up to scald me it would. I learned never to put a cup with liquid in it near him. He became so unpredictable that I'd be fleeing the house first thing in the morning and taking the car to do so, because there is no other way to flee without getting soaked, and it was my car, purchased for my purposes, until Eddie crawled into my life. Plus I was keen to keep him out of my car for very good reasons. He'd been stopped a few times with drink taken. And even though he had rigged up a jalopy of his own from discarded lumps of different cars, he would still swipe mine instead. It was as the Tall Man had trained me: predict and get ahead of the questions. Get up and out into the car before Forty Guts. It was how I became so committed to Meals on Wheels. It gave me a purpose for being in the car.

Now though, I have come home, and when I am home the only safe place for me to be is in the leaba.

A Crustie said something bothersome to me the other day. You spend a lot of time lying down, Bina, says she. Were you always that way or is this recent? You might be depressed, you might be at risk, she said. And I returned her a look that said mind who and what you are asking and give me the bag of food you are delivering and be gone.

I used to be agoraphobic myself, she added swift, but this community has helped me overcome it. *You*, she said, more forcefully, have helped me overcome it.

I believed no such thing.

I have no agoraphobia, I told her, it's only humans I am in here hiding from. I've no problem at all with the open air, if you get rid of all the humans.

Anytime you want to come out and join us you are welcome.

Thank you. Good night, I said. The poor girl was as thick as a post and wasn't hearing a word I was saying to her. I'm saying I don't want to be near humans and she's replying come out to our stinking tent and join us.

I am challenged by these Crusties, but they are very good at doing messages and bringing me pie and if they are to be out there they need to make themselves useful or be scarce.

I didn't like her questions. I didn't like that she noticed. I didn't like that they might be out there sitting up discussing me lying down. I didn't like it, not because I was ashamed of my lying down. I didn't like it because the Tall Man trained me. He had trained me not to draw attention to myself and here I had launched a hundred gold balloons worth of attention and all because of going to bed. But this was what he had long warned. It's the ordinary thing you think won't be noticed, that's what will send them in.[29]

But

Maybe

Now

Here's the thing

Maybe there comes a time in every woman's life to lie down.

Maybe you lie down no matter if someone is abusing you or bothering you or not.

Maybe it was just the time to lie down.

I amn't sure.

Sometimes you aren't sure.

That's not a warning.

It's factual talk.

---

[29] Now I'm thinking on it, wasn't this exactly what the Tall Man did turning up to visit me here the day I came out of prison? He knew they'd not look for him that day because they assumed he'd never come on such an obvious day. Wasn't he clever?

·

She missed her kitchen.
Bina became a stranger in it.
She hadn't realized how much she liked her kitchen
Until she was unwelcome in it.
Chased out.

Bina tried Phil's advice.
She tried to have a conniption.
It was rare Bina took advice
And she intended never to do so again.

·

The conniption didn't work exactly.

But

It didn't exactly fail.

But

It didn't entirely succeed.

But

It wasn't enough of one.

It was a reluctant conniption.

That's a lot of buts, but life is nothing but a ruler-length but. A major trouble was that the daughter of one of the Meals on Wheels cooks saw me and I could hardly lie to her about what I was up to. Hello there Bina, she said as I'd raised a vase up above my head in the home-and-style section of Dunnes Stores. I had to stop the conniption. Before it got going. I only managed to knock over a large lamp and kick a planter. A benign seizure, they said. Go home and sleep. I don't have a bath, I told them before they could tell me to take a hot one.

It is important to get your final exit in order. That's what the Tall Man said to me, early on in the Group endeavour, when he implied I should join them. He went on with his explaining for a long while over an early game of Scrabble. I remember because I was struggling quite hard throughout with a combination of letters I've strangely never gotten since. Many more I's or U's than is useful. I asked him where his interest in the Group had come from.

It was a long story, but since I was now in his confidence—and I had to understand that once I was in his confidence, I would never be out of it and did I understand that? He did not look up on that question, yet he registered my nodded reply and segued straight to more explaining.

His involvement had come from two places. The first and most important, he said, was he was called to serve (I confess I had no clue what he meant, but assumed he received some sort of signal) but his main motivation came from watching his own mother's death. She was taken very bad and a disagreement emerged among his two siblings. *I watched my mother's exhausted eyes. I saw her mouth globbed up with tubes and my pedant brother, who had by now turned heavily to God, insisting none of us could say what my mother wanted. My sister neither agreed nor disagreed, she just stared at our mother and subsequently said it was too distressing to see her in this state and that she could no longer visit her. I said with confidence I knew our mother did not want this. Would you want it?* The Tall

Man said he'd asked his brother. The brother replied he placed his future and his life in the hands of the Lord. And what if the Lord has no definite plan? We had been estranged for years and only our mother's demise threw us together in this room, you must understand. Once inside the room, who makes the decision? Be careful whom you wind up in a room with, he warned me. I thought it was quite excellent advice given the situation I'd already gotten myself in with Eddie.

Oh you've no need to warn me on that front, I said. I have made every mistake possible. He placed down the word "equip" on the Scrabble board and muttered only you must get rid of him.

Easy said.

Be careful whom you invite into your home, my mother warned me, said he.

And yet she wasn't ready herself?

Well she had failed to tally who was already in her room. You have no idea what your children will grow up to become.

Unbearable would be my hardiest guess.

You are not far wrong, he said. Your turn.

The word I played was complacent

I have never since topped it.

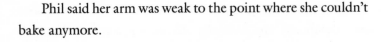

Phil said her arm was weak to the point where she couldn't bake anymore.

You hate baking, I said. You were always complaining about baking.

That's not the point, she said.

Well what is the point?

I could bake. I could bake so I had something to complain about.

I agreed.

I saw her point.

The fact of the matter is it's important to have something to complain about, and if it is baking so be it.

I would never want to live in a country where complaining was forbidden.

What would you talk of, if it were so?

One winter during Eddie, we were hit with awful bad weather

And things deteriorated.

It snowed.

That was unusual.

It was very, very cold. It's usually very, very cold in my house. I kept it cold deliberately to tempt Eddie to leave.

It was during this cold spell my daily escape plans could work no longer.

We were penned in

Eddie and I

And things unravelled.

Or maybe they finally came together.

Because ultimately it trampolined his arse out of here.

There are too many coincidences for the power of prayer not to have worked, a very sick woman once said to me as I helped her, in the way that I have been helping people, but cannot specify how here. For if I write it down, people will suffer. I don't want suffering. I don't want more Eddie. I want it to stop. I want the man or woman who has had enough to be able to go for a sleep without end, for I have known intermittently what it is to desire that and I haven't even had the agony of physical pain boring 76 holes in my head all day long. If it was the power of prayer that brought me to her, and the relief I honestly only-by-chance delivered—since there are a few of us in the Group—so be it. I am not a one-woman bandit like the papers insist. How, I asked her, could she be certain that what we were about to do was the right thing for her to do?

I have prayed about it, she said.

But God would be frowning on what you propose here?

I have prayed for him to send me a signal to proceed. And he has sent me you.

I handed her the small paper cup with the flowers on it and gave her the talk that we must give. That if you. Then this will. And are you understanding me?

Oh I am, she said. I've never understood any single thing better.

She was the only person I ever witnessed who downed it

all in one swig and did not plead for chocolate or apple juice nor cough or spit.

Her head went back onto that pillow.

She smiled peacefully.

Mouthed the words thank you.

I held her hand.

Good night now, I said.

She squeezed my hand.

All's well, I said.

I was there.

She was there.

It was indisputable when the time for reckoning came.

The pipes froze

During the very cold spell.

We had no heat.

Eddie and I were stuck inside the house with no hot water and no ability to escape each other.

He received an awful lot of phone calls. People seemed to be angry with him about not picking up or dropping off stuff. He said he couldn't get up the hill but he'd get it gone soon. He spoke in lowered mumbles and, given he was unable to speak in a normal tone of voice and usually always shouted, I confess I was suspicious about what he was up to.

It was then that I realized Eddie had the potential to kill me.

He could kill me rapid or continue to erode me slowly as he had been doing.

When we weren't frozen in
I could duck
I could dodge.

I could remove myself to bed or remove myself from the house, but as long as he remained, I was at risk. I understood, like I never could have envisaged possible, why someone would want to take a shortcut and be gone. I understood because a lump like Eddie can be very hard to move. It is simply a fact that as long as he kept coming home, I was at his mercy. The only reasonable prospect of escape was to not be alive anymore and never face dealing with him again.

I'd do well to heed my own advice when I'm declaring Phil was wrong.

I'd do well to heed my own warnings

But who amongst us ever heeds our own advice.

We issue the decree

And the day following forget whatever was decreed and boil the person an egg.

During the most unbearable years of Eddie, I pressed the Group to allow me to help those furthest away from my home. I had good reasons. If there were a few visits involved, it would take me time to go there and back and keep me out of the house and supply a pause or period of peace, for which I was desperate. I would need the car and I could take the car with confidence knowing that if I hesitated someone else would suffer. I will tell you in the suffering that has been dealing with that man I have found great comfort in relieving the suffering of others.[30]

I vividly recall, during those two weeks of frozen pipes and no heat, the desire to walk west into the sky. To literally walk inside the sky and become enveloped, bamboozled and made dizzy by cloud. I could feel or imagine how cold the cloud might be and it was a great comfort. That fierce cuddle of cold cloud. Transporting, actually.

Such imaginings may well have been assisted by the fact it was −9 outside and about −14 inside. It took me a couple of days to realize how bad this was. We rarely had such cold weather and I was unprepared. It's hard to be prepared when you've spent years fleeing your home daily, just to conserve

---

[30] It could be said that he delivered me unto it. I might say this in the court, that if anyone should be on trial it should be Eddie. But they wouldn't heed me. No one listens to me.

some sanity. Eventually you've no idea what's happening inside your home or what you are coming home to, never mind adding the interference of arctic weather.

Fuck there's no water, said Eddie.

Fuck there's no hot water either, said Eddie.

Fuck it's freezing cold, Eddie said.

Fuck the heat's not working neither.

And he looked at me with the wholesale expectation I could solve all of it. And when I wasn't able to give him any kind of response he began banging and stomping about and violently pushing things off the table, and I really became afraid when he punched his fist into the hallway wall. Directly into a glass photo frame. I was so frightened I can't even now bring myself to recall who was located inside the frame. Yet I must have repaired it. Picked up and out the glass and seen whose face stared back at me. But it's all gone. All that remains is that strongest of memories: I was trapped inside my home with a violent man, who was very angry that the heat had failed us. And what it means to be trapped in a confined space with such a man. And the bald, uncomfortable truth that not only had I invited him in, I'd physically conducted him in.

On and on he tiraded that I was a stupid cunt and how could I not even fucking manage to put fucking heat on like every other cunt-fuck in this village and wasn't I some . . . on and on, it bled and unwound. His anger came from no specific location and yet it could become an urban settlement of rage in 60 seconds. The words scared me less than his sounds. The anger of displaced objects being flipped off a surface. The kick of his boot into my sideboard and the crashing of the three cups that fell down and smashed. Which cups were they,

I wondered, under the crunch of his hoof as he walked on them and stamped them further to smithereens. Then another hurl let out of him and the sound of cup fragments being kicked further across the floor. But the repeated sound that stayed with me was always his fist. I never recovered from that first time he punched me straight into my ear. I never heard right since on that side, in that ear. And to this day I am none the wiser as to why he landed that first punch at all.

She found herself looking at his hands and wondering would be they be good at fiddling locks and entering small windows.

When she heard someone local had their house broke into Bina wondered would Eddie be capable.

Probably.

She wondered if he was the sort of man who might club an old person over the head with a brick and then come home here and quietly put the kettle on.

He might.

Would Eddie club her over the head?

He might.

Would that make all matters simpler?

It might.

That's a terrible thought, but if she were to die by another's hand, it mightn't be all bad.

And now she thought about it, it might be very handy.

She won't lie to you

Bina started doing something that surprised her.

She began watching what Eddie brought into the house

To see were there clues

There weren't.

The room just smelt bad when she took a look around it.

She repeatedly stood in the doorway and wondered how do you get rid of such a man?

You start a fire, a voice told her.

She remembered a story in the paper about a woman who lit the family chip shop on fire because she said she was sick of the smell of it and everyone had gotten health conscious and it was only drunk people eating chips.

The problem was she also burnt out the hairdressers beside it and half of the Centra and Doireann's dress shop too. People said nobody bought anything much at Doireann's dress shop, but that wasn't what Doireann said tearfully on the news. She said her family business had been destroyed and she was destroyed and several families' school uniforms were also destroyed. Doireann stood in front of her ruined shop. A plump man with his shirt misbuttoned said it was an absolute disgrace and that whoever the culprit was would be found and made accountable with the full force of the law.

Bina wondered what use is the full force of the law within homes where the light doesn't let the law look in.

Starting fires wasn't a good idea
Even to get rid of an Eddie.

She discussed the idea with Phil, which she would come to regret.

But the thought did stay with her.

She won't lie about that.

She won't lie about how often she considered letting a match fall to the floor beside something discarded.

If she left the house for a reason, she could merely have been distracted.

Sometimes she thought of other things

Like how easy it is to leave people miserable and at the mercy of those who are miserable to them.

Stop Bina.

Stop it.

If you write out everything you think

They'll think it's everything you did.

Rather than everything you thought about doing.

And they are already too interested in what you didn't do.

●

Always have a chat to yourself before you think of doing something.

Like stealing a car or lighting a fire or acting the eejit around a lamp post.

A chat can put a stop to it.

That's all we'll say now on that.

A retroactive warning.

There may be others.

I did worry I gave Phil notions when I talked about the fire-lighting idea

That I was guilty of that

And should get 14 years for discussing the idea with her

But I never said she should light herself on fire.[31]

---

[31] The Solicitor wants to discuss self-immolation with me. What is your interest in self-immolation about? Come again, I said, what is it?

I thought so, he said

No further questions.

I wouldn't.

It was Eddie needed shifting, not Phil.

Phil was great company even when she was moaning and deluded.

I loved that woman.

I loved that woman in all her moaning delusion

And her ascending and collapsing blood sugars

And now she's gone

And that's very, very wrong.

I did tell Eddie there were angry men looking for him

And he should watch his back.

He ignored me and went back to sending texts.

I continued to drop hints about angry men as I delivered Meals on Wheels so that if ever I took any action I'd have laid a trail of crumbs towards Eddie himself.

I learned about laying crumbs in a pointed direction from the Tall Man.

His training was useful that way.

And I want to be very clear, he was only helping people.

I had no intention of further helping Eddie.

My only intention was to eject him.

In a form that would not fail, for I was finished with failure.

I won't lie to you.

The Tall Man began to disconcert me. I've to admit now it's the rare man who *doesn't* disconcert me, but I was surprised to find myself growing suspicious of him.

He, the Tall Man, was so, how can I put it, taut. He, or his brain or his emotions or whatever you want to call what was going on in his upstairs chamber, was like a rubber band that never stretched or adjusted itself. It always fit. Whatever the situation, he maintained a calm detachment. I could see it was necessary, his demeanour, to undertake the task and administer the help he was providing and I'll say this here and I'd say it loudly in your ear: I never stood in any kitchen, bathroom or bedroom where I was in any shadow of a doubt he wasn't providing much needed relief, for the second he ceased to do so, I would have been gone.

I told a lie.

I told a lie above.

There has been one man who did not disconcert me and his name was Tomás. I never had a moment uncomfortable or unwelcome in his company. If I took cold spuds in to him I was welcome. If I took no spuds in to him I was welcome. If I took the worst rice pudding and relieved him of 5 euros for doing so, I was welcome. I also never met a man who took the amount of comfort that man did in the delivery of the right cup of tea.

It's three bags isn't it? he'd say to me as we debated the volume of tea that had to go into the pot to achieve what we both knew to be the right cup of tea.

I think it is. I think it takes three bags these days to get it right.

And every time he'd take the first swig, and it wasn't easy for him to swig with his swallowing problems, but every time we would discuss whether it was the right cup of tea and if it wasn't quite right I'd make it again, but it was rare to never I'd have to make it a third time.

He explained it had long been a source of tension between himself and his elusive brother,[32] who was supposed to be taking care of him but was rarely to be seen. The brother took umbrage at the volume of tea Tomás used or asked to be used in the teapot and would make only the weakest of tea. It is pure shite the tea that fella makes and I can't get to the kettle so easy to fix it, Tomás complained. The wrong cup of tea can make a body very miserable. It's not that you'd need the right cup of tea all day long. You can bypass a few cups. An average or passable six of them. But about every twelve there's a long thirst only ever relieved by the right cup. Am I right?

Oh you are. You're absolutely right.

And I'll tell you now it was the very rare time I'd find myself in agreement with any man at all. And here I was not

---

[32] Eddie's father's twin brother. Another great man for avoiding Eddie. He'd hardly been seen since Eddie's accident, terrified he'd be scuttled with him because he was his father's twin.

just endorsing Tomás but lifting his cup and going into his kitchen in pursuit of the right cup of tea he had so wonderfully articulated for me and not just for him, but for the pair of us. Because it was sharing that near perfect cup of tea with him that gave me the calmest moments of my week, where for a brief instant I could imagine I would one day be free of Eddie.

Much of my reluctance about helping to extinguish Tomás was that I had such comfort from visiting him and, were he to be gone, it would be one less place to flee to from Eddie. I didn't like to burden him with this fact, so I left it unsaid.

And he'd begin again with the talk of *people like us*. He and I, why was it we weren't rewarded with children, and did I think it was timing or was it God's decision and were some chosen and some not. I said no. I thought it was nothing to do with timing but rather that some of us had more sense and could avoid a bucket of trouble being sloshed into our laps.

I knew it was an unsatisfactory answer. I knew it then and I know it now. And what would have been the truth? The truthful answer was: Tomás, I have saddled myself with a belly full of a troubled adult (what's worse, one related to you) and here I am escaping in your home the very mess I created, while fictitiously claiming a calm I do not possess. But what would have been the good in disappointing him? None whatsoever. I wanted him instead to take up the determination to carry on living. To continue to exist. Crucially to be here so I had someone to visit so I could get away from Eddie.

But why should someone I had a tenuous connection to be expected to carry on living a life of pure misery so I could be unburdened from my own self-induced misery? It was a void transaction and I knew it. I could have and should have told him, but I wasn't trained that way. What way was I trained? I'll tell you the way. The way that you are trained. You, who are reading this and nodding at the warnings in recognition. Nodding too late at the warnings. Nodding too late at this warning, knowing there's someone who is not just on your sofa or in your back bedroom, but has probably commandeered both. That's a fact. And then there are those reading and thinking, isn't she daft, why didn't she walk or why didn't she do this or that. Well I am not worried about you, because maybe you've had the good fortune to be trained different and would not scupper yourself this way. And isn't it as well for you.

I wish she'd shut up.
I bet that's what you're thinking.
Know this much
Know it firm
Know it tall
Know it wide
I will not shut up
I will not shut up at all.
For once I am outside my door
I don't shut up.
Inside is another story

For I had a lingering desire to keep a set of ears on me
And Eddie would cut them off me given half a chance.
So if you are listening to a woman
Hoping she'll shut up
Try imagining the 2,000 years
Where she did all the listening.
Sit down
Shut up
And if the woman is talking, listen.

That's not a warning
It's a command.
There won't be many commands here.
But that's one of them.

However
If she is talking utter rubbish
You can make your excuses
For much rubbish is sprayed about regardless of your
gender or your body parts
But if she is talking and saying nothing
There's sometimes a lot being said
Listen into the gaps of what's not being said and you'll
find your answer.

Some of Tomás's face had been removed because of the cancer. But he didn't scare me. Not at all. He was just a bit lopsided-looking and could only hear in one ear since the other was missing. What scared me was how he could choke or fall out of bed or be stranded and desperate and have no one to help him back up. His brother[33] was supposed to be caring for him and was collecting a carer's allowance for doing nothing, including never stepping near him. Tomás claimed he could cope to anyone who suggested otherwise. He wouldn't wear the alarm around his neck. He wouldn't depend on anyone. He was glad to see me at his door. I was glad to be at his door. He was glad, I was glad. I worried about him and I hope to God I gave him nothing to worry about.

I did give him my phone number.

I gave it to him because I wanted him to phone. If he phoned for any reason, I could get away from Eddie. I would say it was an emergency.

It was hard though to get him to phone.

He wasn't the phoning sort.

---

[33] Eddie's father's twin. Still avoids Eddie 100% of the time. Phoned me the other day to ask where was Eddie. I said gone to Canada. He said he owes me money, could I ring him. I cannot, I said. He's yours. Ring him yourself.

He wasn't the alarm-pressing sort.

Wasn't he savvy though, for whatever sort I thought him, I remain convinced it was he sent the Tall Man. I still wonder how he did that. It can only be he who sent him.

I did help him.

I helped him because he asked me to help him

I helped him because you would have helped him

I helped him because I think he sent the Tall Man

And it was the Tall Man who asked for my help on behalf of Tomás.

Tomás never asked me direct.

He didn't need to.

He was such a good man. You wouldn't see him suffer. He was easy to help. Honest to God. It was easy not to inflict Eddie on him, which would have been the alternative. He was as decent a man as ever could walk this earth and I helped him because, contrary to what you may hear in court or read in the papers, I am not a mad woman with a syringe. I value decency. I value dignity and I value a good friend.

I might not have known him as long as I knew Phil.

But I couldn't see him suffer

Because I could never relieve his burdens the way I could pretend to myself I was a comfort to Phil.

I couldn't relieve his burdens because our genders provided a degree of separation that Phil and I would never experience.

I could have handled Phil in any condition. I knew that. She didn't know that, or more accurately she didn't want that, and if I could lay my hand across my chest as I write this I would, but I cannot, because if I do you won't be able to read it, but I will say it was her right not to want it.

I was attached to the idea she'd call out to me.

I was attached to the idea I could relieve her burdens.

And I couldn't.

It is my failing.

I'll die knowing that.

Let me say this, let me keep it short and let me not keep you very much longer: If there were a way I could bleed my voice into Phil's still-living ear, I would tell her in the most knowing way she was wrong and that the job was mine to relieve her suffering and comfort her. That is the job of a friend. That is the role of friendship. And that she didn't permit me. She didn't permit me to take her and mind her. And by reply she might tell me to pipe down or if she wasn't feeling so aggressive she might chime no, no, no, not at all, in that sweet upper register of hers that was often reassuring and comforting to the rest of us. Because the thing about Phil is she never wanted to be anybody's burden. I am alone now, she'd say. Now that Jimmy is gone. It is over for me and finished. I've no one left to live for. Jimmy was her son. She was devoted to him. When he was killed in the army she took it awful bad. She took it as a form of beckoning. She held out or held on for as long as she could. But no matter which way I shape it or rephrase it here, she was still wrong. We need you Phil. We needed you Phil. We needed you to carry on. You were wrong and you should have carried on. You don't know who needs you til you're gone. This is the trouble.

Why Phil, though?
Why are you so sure about Phil, Bina?
About Phil's staying?
These are questions I do ask myself.
I just am and you are going to have to take it from me.
OK
Grand.

Of course it's grand, there's no one could argue me under the table on Phil, only the woman herself and she's moved along to better things.

Allegedly.[34]

I'd ask the Tall Man, but he is nowhere to be found.
Nothing strange there.
He had warned while training me that he'd disappear.
Do you know how long I'd serve if I were caught?
I'd never see daylight, he said.
That answered it.

---

[34] Would she ever send a signal and let me know? There's a thing now about the afterlife: all this devotion and no one ever sent me a signal from the beyond. Did they send you one?

███████ phoned and said the Tall Man had shot himself.

Interesting, I said.

And was it in his mouth, the back of his head or under his chin?

She changed the subject.

I knew she was lying

Because I think she was the Mole.

I knew a Mole would have to lie

Because she would need a neat ending.

I'm not for neat endings.

The Tall Man would never shoot himself

Because the Tall Man had no interest in being dead.

The Solicitor said the tape is damning and will damage us.

There's no us, I thought. There's no us at all. There will never be an us. There will be a bill and there is me.

It's not me on the tape, I said. They'll have to search long and hard to find a damning tape of me doing anything other than dropping off trays for Meals on Wheels and lying in bed.

You are the one who is here, he replied. The other fella[35] is gone.

How the tape became damning of me I didn't intend to understand. Do you want to see it? he asked. Certainly not, I said.

I've much better ways to be wasting time than watching tapes.

The Solicitor returned to his babble about co-operation and interviews and said he'd need to be present at every interview. Unless you co-operate, he said.

How many ways are there to say to this man that the co-operation he's after is impossible because I have no information.

I'll co-operate when they find a tape that has me on it. They have nothing on me.

What about the glass in the bag? said he.

But I put down the phone as my answer.

You have to stop hanging up the phone. He was firm.

Lookit I am awful sorry, I said, but the phone dropped.

It's dropping a bit too often, came back his noticing.

The Tall Man trained me well. If you like, he trained me tall. He said leave no tracks. He said talk in riddles. He said eventually they give up.

---

[35] He speaks of the Tall Man. Actually he said his name. I had to shout at him to be quiet. He was very confused. It's very truculent between us.

They were not giving up.

They were not giving up because I was a woman and I was grabable.

In some situations, dire ones, the Tall Man said ending your life would be a reasonable solution. Like the woman who set the chip shop on fire, I thought. Did I ever tell you the end of that story?

Well, once the charred ruins of them four buildings were revealed, it became clear the woman from the chip shop was responsible. She went missing, the papers said. She is missing, the papers said. Find her, the papers read.

Those statements chased her into the sea.

Poor lamb.

Whatever about the smell that was bothering her, a cold death is a nasty one.

Once she was dead, people were sympathetic.

They said it was unnecessary. That she'd made a mistake, but nobody should be driven to take their life. The Tall Man even mentioned the story of the chip-shop woman. He likely told me the story of the chip-shop woman to illustrate what to do when I found myself in the situation I now find myself in.

He did this because he knew he'd be putting me in this situation.

The day I took the card out of my purse and looked at it and couldn't remember what to do with it, that was the day, the minute, the moment I could briefly see Phil's point of view. I could see why she might be right. My dawning moment. My indisputable minute, if you like, and I'll warn you, you're going to have many of them but there will be one you'll remember until you don't remember.[36] And the saddest part of all is, at that point, there is no one whatsoever to remember for you and so I am warning you here and now to write it down. All of it. Record it the way I am here or they'll make it up on your behalf, the people who go about making things up, like Phil's angry daughters. Never have daughters, they get into your knicker drawer and make a mess. Did I already tell you that? See if it's noted above. I can go back and check in a minute. Always make a note someplace. Shove it up your sleeve, in your pocket, down your sock, but carry that slip of paper always. I still recall my moment of not recalling because I am not yet quite in the condition by which I can no longer write to you. My moment did pass. But it has not wholly passed. Just fragmented. I put the card back into my purse and set the purse aside. And under my watch is a small piece of paper stuck, it says bank card in tiny writing. I put the same note into my coat pocket with *take out money* on the reverse. A small message that reminds me I did not know what to do with my bank card. That was the first

---

[36] And then we'll have lost you.

sign, truth be told. And if you've someone useful nearby you can tell them where it is recorded, so they can retrieve it for that interview they will give you when you stop remembering enough for them to start noticing *all* that you forget.

More's the pity you don't get to select which parts you'd like to forget quicker, for I know what I'd choose and at this stage you too probably know what I'd choose.

Because if I haven't succeeded in conveying that much to you, put this whole pile of papers into the fire.

After Eddie.
What you'll remember.
What you'll regret.
What you'll never quite know.

Can you imagine if eulogies told the truth of a person? He was rancid and awful and needed a good clout. I wish he'd died sooner and faster and left me in peace. I am glad to see the back of him, bar the door on both sides, back and front in heaven. Don't let him in. Or, she ruined my sheets and there was never a clean cup in the house. She yowled and howled and shat and spat and I am glad the horror is over. Or, she was alright. Nothing special. There needs to be a *won't be missed* list to go with all these poems and clever rhymes on remembering.

Remarkings

My name is still Bina and these are my remarkings.

Remarkings are different from warnings.

But you will find warnings within the remarkings

If you are careful enough to notice them.

And if you don't, I can't help you.

It's how it has to be.

I've had to mix them in now.

I've had to speed up.

Time is against me.

There was a woman.
There was briefly a woman.
And God love that woman
Whom I won't name.
I still pray for her
There's not a day I don't think about her.

Eddie had a woman.
This is the woman of whom I write.
I felt bad and glad for her
Glad because she might get Eddie gone
Bad because if she took him on
She was due a very terminal life.
I tried to be warm with her
While I also tried to warn her with my eyes
And
Grimaces.
Small smiles
Tight ones.

The Unfortunate is what I'll call her, since she might wish never to be reminded of the six weeks she spent near that forty-gutted rupture of a man. She might have it assigned as a dreadful migraine that finally passed. Never to be revisited or remembered. Scorched out.

The Unfortunate was useful and kind

Thoughtful

Deliberate

In her actions

In her intentions

This woman

Who had the misfortune to temporarily attach herself to Eddie.

There was no one much around these parts to interest her.

Her stoicism was her biggest trial

And her warmth

She should have surrendered that soonest.[37]

Eddie was abysmal

He'd bark vaguely at her.

Tell her to take things

Items.

Get. Give. Hand me. Hurry.

Tell her to bring things to incomprehensible destinations and then claim he'd said leave it by the gate.

He constantly asked her where things were, as though she were a walking inventory of everything he'd touched, seen or ever thought about, long before she even existed.

This is the thing about Eddies.

Eddies have everyone running around after them, serving them, fetching for them, and when something is needed for someone other than themselves they are nowhere to be

---

[37] Go cold on them. Go cold on the chancer who might wrap himself around your legs. Or have his hand inside your purse.

found. They are geniuses at selfishly shelving themselves out of the way.

I did try to intercede
And then I stopped.
Because
Soon enough he had the two of us run wide.
And me cooking extra food for her
And her refusing to eat
And wanting to be no bother
And when she was bothered
We were both bothered
We were so bothered
The two of us
By Eddie.
I will be truthful
Are you ready for this?
I did pray Eddie would die during the time in which the Unfortunate was around
I had a novena of Masses offered with this intention
I atoned by sending word above that I would take the Unfortunate in and house her instead.
If the Lord could relieve us of Eddie
I could imagine her bereft
And me baking things to make her feel better
While silently knowing between the mashed-up pastry folds
We were both far better off
Now Eddie was buried.
Except Eddie is not buried.

Others are buried
Phil is buried
Because Phil was wrong
And that will get you buried.
I have noticed that it's the decent people who are buried
While it's the parasites and demolishers who endure.
Hence it's well worth joining the dead
Rather than remaining
To only more mashing and din.

But why?
Why didn't I release myself from Eddie, given the means
I had to do it, what with the Group and the Tall Man.
But
See
Here
Now
That's the difference between
Murder
&
Mercy.

The Group are for mercy
Not murder

You couldn't contradict that.
I intend to say it in the court
But I may not have the chance.
You'd be surprised how little is said in court
of any consequence
This has surprised me.
By the time the Judge finally has a chat with you
It's over and all decided
And he/she looks at you cross
And says you shouldn't have done it
And that's not the time to start saying
Well, you know, Your Honour,
Maybe there are a few things we could talk about out the
back
Or over a bun.

If Phil knew
Where I am now standing
She would see
She was wrong.
Are you listening, Phil?
Because you should be.
I hope the two ears are roasting on you.
Wherever you are.
I hope your lobes are singed hot beneath the soil.

He talked at her.

Eddie talked at Bina.

Loudly

Non-stop

He planned aloud what would never happen.

Like progress.

Eddie couldn't talk in a normal voice.

Most people cannot talk in a normal voice if they are stocious drunk but Eddie couldn't manage normal even at 9 o'clock in the morning.

He shouted.

He was always shouting.

He shouted when he was asking me to turn on the kettle.

He shouted even to tell me the day looked warm.

I imagined he was deaf because I prefer that to the truth he was ignorant.

Because he never listened if you told him anything.

He just shouted.

Eventually I stopped listening.

I had to.

No sane person could actually listen to his slop and remain sane.

That voice was like a lawnmower inside my ear
finding nothing to mow but stones.

They say they have evidence

Evidence against me

Evidence from Eddie.

Someone phoned and warned me. I don't remember if it was ▓▓▓▓▓ or not as I stopped answering all phone calls and the messages mounted and blunted into a big blur of voice. I did this because I knew it would force the Solicitor to come to my door.

I don't know why I wanted to bring him to my door to deliver the news, but I can be stubborn this way. I think he knew I was doomed. I knew I was doomed and I wanted to look at his face for confirmation. I was weary of third-hand phone calls from some poor young one appointed to blather at me.

•

Nobody is telling the truth. Nobody is telling the truth about the new evidence.

That's what Bina thinks.

•

And it's very annoying.

The way people do this to old people

Especially when they are accusing you of murdering someone.

Especially when you're facing 14 years for aiding, abetting or counselling.

Who knew a conversation could get you 14 years?

I should have known.

I'd already seen this with Eddie.

It was a conversation that lumbered me with Eddie to begin with.

Phil said she suspected Forty Guts deliberately crashed his motorbike into my wall.

There are people who do it.

Do what?

Crash into your car or your wall to get the insurance money.

Why didn't he just knock at the door & rob me?

Because you'd never let him in if he came to the door.

She was right.

Phil was right

And it's very hard for me to record this. My hand is trembling with resistance, but it must be writ.

I have wondered about many things.

A lifetime of wondering and waiting has led me only to wonder even more, all over the back of these bills and papers. To wonder how much, how much longer and how much worse. And this is why I have ceased and lain down. The worry of wondering has me flattened.

I have wondered how Tomás knew to send the Tall Man to me

I have wondered how he found the Tall Man.

I have wondered about both.

I have wondered whether Tomás knew I was still housing his nephew Eddie and whether he wanted to be gone, so as to not face him, or was his intention that I put Eddie into his house once he was gone? Maybe he thought that in going he'd relieve me of Eddie.

I have wondered if Eddie knew I helped Tomás.

This is what worried me most.

I had to help Tomás have his exit without impediment.

I had to put up with Eddie for fear he had information on that very exit.

You could not send Eddie into a house with a man who'd lost half his face and all his dignity, who was living quietly, but living in dreadful pain. He lived quietly for a very good reason. He didn't want to go into a nursing home, didn't want to bring attention to the fact he couldn't physically cope. He let it be thought his other brother[38] was there with him. For all I know he told them Eddie was there too. He lived quietly because he was determined not to die loudly. He was too proud to die loud and disgruntled, with an abundance of fuss and prayers. He was right about that.

I think perhaps he knew I was holding Eddie back from him and his way of appreciating it was his intention for Eddie to go into his house once he was dead.

It was strange how that worked out.

Eddie wouldn't go.

Eddie had no intention of moving.

Sure why would he move?

He felt himself in charge here.

He had colonized my home & land to suit himself

And filled it with an amount of rubbish no solid nation would tolerate.

I was focused on Eddie not knowing

Not knowing I had helped Tomás.

And then there was still the other brother

Tomás hadn't imagined how many brothers turn up

After the fact.

---

[38] Not the dead brother, Eddie's father. Another brother. It gets very complicated with all these brothers I'm sorry. There are eight of them in that family. All avoiding each other. I can't keep track of them.

The other brother is in there now full-time. Would you believe?

Of course you would

Why wouldn't you.

He, who wouldn't go near the man alive, is living full-time in Tomás's bed now it's empty. Now he can find his way to the bed alright, and the part I wonder about is each night when he puts his head down: Does it occur to him to consider the man who lay there before, the man he barely set eyes on, the man to whom he never passed a cup, the man he lied about to the Health Board and insisted he was helping so he could collect a carer's allowance for not caring, and fuel allowance for leaving him cold and roaring. Ah but now. Ah here well. You can conjure up all the splutter you want across counters and up on bar stools. You'll say I was the problem because I didn't make it difficult for the brother not to call into him, and that if I hadn't gone in to Tomás the brother would have, but do you honestly think Tomás would have been pleading with me for help to exit if what was coming into him of his own flesh and blood was a good reason to keep on living? It wasn't. But see, if I write that here I will be accused of all sorts. I cannot keep up with the allegations. They are coming clipping at me like tennis balls. The authorities have looked around my house at benign and useless implements and given them a cause and purpose they've never had. They've made a mad old show happen in here, where there was nothing other than a sad old one. The sad show of a woman who was sunk by what she invited in and forced out each day to avoid it. Out there I was full of perk and shout about who should and shouldn't do this or that to you. I was a great woman for delivering the verdicts to others that I could neither conjure or conquer for myself. Within these four walls it was persistence, it was never living. And it is for those people who, through no fault of their own, weren't living that I persisted and helped. I did for others what no one could have done for me. And as I had insufficient courage to banish Eddie, my own hand would have rounded on myself eventually—had the cold hand of the law not cleverly come for me first.

How it is.

That's how it is.

For all of us

Really.

I am glad Eddie is gone

I want only that he not come back

The only assurance of that is to be gone myself.

Morbid

But

True.

Pure. Factual. Talk.

Don't forget

Eddie built the yard on top of me.

I think he planned to bury me in it

To disappear me that way

But soon the neighbours started complaining and grew suspicious.

They would have noticed if I'd gone away

They let him know that.

Then

Items became stranger and stranger

That arrived.

I longed to tell whoever was giving him stuff to stop.

Could you tell whoever is filling up the back with their rubbish to stop?

What's that?

What's that stuff mounting up there?

My machines, Eddie said. That's all mine.

Well move it?

It's moving. People are buying it all. It's all sold, Eddie said. Everything out there is sold.

I took a walk back there alone and examined it all. It was much worse than it looked from the window. I counted 42 tires, which made me very unhappy. There were three broken paddling pools for children, one had an elephant in it. There were tables, chairs, empty cases, tea chests, there were even a few toilet bowls up there. There were at least three baths. One of them looked like it had been attacked by an axe. There was a car seat from a Renault 4 that had a big slash in it. All of it was outside. All of it was in my garden. All of it had been rained on. The car batteries really confused and frightened me so I wasn't going to stand for them.

Get rid of the batteries, I told him. Whatever about the pink sofa and the toilet bowls, I am having no car batteries lying about up here. Get them gone or you'll be gone. It was the first time I'd used a determined note of exit with him. (Car batteries will do that to me. I don't like them.)

Wha? What's that? he repelled me. Oh them. I'm only minding them for a fella.

Well tell him to come and remove them or I'll call the council and they'll remove both you and the batteries, I said.

I told Eddie stop with the bonfires.
I told Eddie the bonfires had to stop
The flames were too high.
I was worried they'd burn us all.

●

Bina couldn't be absolutely certain where Eddie's fires were being burnt.

Eddie was lighting them on common land beside her field.

Common land meant she had no business asking him to stop.

If you want rid of the rubbish you'll have to accept bonfires.

Eddie made it sound like Bina had created all the rubbish.

Stop collecting rubbish, she said.

He said the fires were part of his business.

●

No more stuff back there, I said, you have the place destroyed. He muttered raméis about a man needing space to do his man's work uninterrupted and how did I think the bills would be paid around here? That was when it dawned on me he was off his head entirely, as he'd never paid a bill in the years he had lived here. Nor was he ever likely to.

". . . skips were found containing building rubble, kitchen units, window frames and a sunbed," the report read.

Eddie lied about the skip. First he said the skip was there for us to clear out the house and *his yard*, as he'd begun calling my back garden, and that he'd be filling it up and a friend would be collecting it. The skip seemed to come and go, but nothing ever left the land and the skip seemed to return refilled each time.

Eddie said I wasn't to worry.

Everything was sold and people were coming to collect it and he'd be building a fence so I wouldn't have to look at it since it was upsetting me.

Eddie had changed his tack.

He was shouting less, but I did not believe this new softy mumble he was trying.

Sure enough

Soon enough

He was shouting again.

Eddie said I was very unreasonable and obstructing him.

Eddie said I didn't want him to make progress.

Eddie said I was the problem.

Eddie said so much gabbling grunt it was easy to forget what he said.[39]

I finally realized the best thing was to say nothing to Eddie[40]

Because as soon as I spoke to him

A headache would come over me for three days

And I'd never really had bad headaches like this.

The equation was simple:

---

[39] If I am asked in the court it'll be awkward.

[40] He was very unreliable.

Talk to Eddie

Get a headache.

Don't talk to Eddie

Eddie is a headache.

Did I want to double my headaches?

No I did not.

Eddie seemed increasingly excited and galvanized by his plans.

He built a fence

It was crooked and ugly.

Temporary, he said.

It was temporary.

To stop me being upset.

One night I heard a noise out there

And was surprised when I stepped out

To see what looked like a digger waving its bucket at me.

I wasn't going to go over and investigate because it was dark and raining and because there had been a few break-ins in the area and people were afraid of getting murdered.

The next day I did ask him.

Oh it was just parked. Just parking. A fella was parking it there overnight.

He was on a job nearby. And Eddie was helping him.

It sounded like Eddie was being useful for the first time ever, so I said no more about it.

I was curious though, so I had a look around where I recalled the digger had been and where Eddie may have been digging in the middle of the night.

I wasn't sure what or why he was digging.

I wasn't sure that I wanted to find out.

Phil said if Eddie was digging, why wouldn't he make himself useful and bury himself in the process.

We both laughed.

You don't think?

What? That he's buried someone?

God no, I said. Eddie is too big of an eejit to manage that. He's up to something but it's unlikely to be murder.

You've to get shut of him, Phil said.

I know, I said. But it's not that easy.

I'll tell you what's easy, Phil said. But she lost her train of thought, became distracted and never finished the sentence.

It was what was happening to the two of us in different ways. Our minds would wander but we'd reassure one another we were as sharp as ever while individually knowing we were not. One reassuring the other would cancel out the misery of the one needing to be reassured and it was the dance we did. Heel and toe and side to side and back and forth and she and I.

Find me the woman who wouldn't help her friend?

I can tell you this: I know no such a woman, but whoever she is cannot be living a happy life. For what is there other than the comfort of each other? Even in delusion and collusion there needs to be a woman to tell another woman, go way out of that, you're alright. It's how it is. How would you carry on without it? I'll tell you how. You'd be Eddie and I wouldn't wish that on any man or woman.

Tomás is why I took Eddie in at all.

Tomás was his uncle. Eddie had no other family in the area and I'd assumed he'd return to whomever he belonged to in Waterford[41] before he flew into my ditch.[42] After a few weeks' recovery, I assumed he'd be right and ready, once he finished his rehab. He had to be near the hospital for his physio and I was near enough and could get him there. I never really thought beyond a few weeks and I knew very well Tomás couldn't take him in. I had Eddie taken in, really, before I discussed it properly with Tomás, who told me straight to *get rid of him at the earliest chance Bina as he is nothing but a bellyful. I'll tell you the truth, that if he had arrived intact at my door, I would have pretended not to be home and if he'd got a cup of tea out of me*

---

[41] Or whomever he owed money to in Waterford.

[42] I'd better start writing the truth: before he crashed his motorbike DELIBERATELY into my wall and landed in my ditch.

he'd have been as lucky. So didn't he land very well on the top of his head outside your house, because if it were me he'd have been left out there on the top of his head. I wish you'd spoken to me, was what Tomás repeatedly said. *He'll take advantage of you. He's an awful fella. He's an oaf, I tell ya.*

I lied to Tomás and told him Eddie was leaving.
I might even have told him Eddie had left.
I didn't want to worry him.
Meanwhile I was visiting him mostly to escape from Eddie.
Tomás was my respite.

And wasn't I an awful fool.
I was and I am.
And that's why I am putting all my foolishness down here, on full display, for you to learn and pay heed to.
Eddie had no mother. She died. His father was killed more recent, 20 years ago, in a farming accident in Waterford and it was on the news. We all felt bad for the boy who'd already lost his mother. He took it hard, it was said. Knowing what I knew by then of Tomás and his situation, I knew the last thing he could tolerate was Eddie inside with him, and it was less damage to me to let him in than to let him go back at his very

ill uncle again. And wasn't I the fool now I lie here thinking on it. For Tomás is dead and I am destroyed and Eddie would have killed him anyway.

Sacrifice is a stupid thing that women do.

Don't do it.

The men don't notice.

And all the women around you spend their lives mopping you up.

So you're only making more and more work for the women who'll have to repair you.

That's more than a warning

It is an order.

Be prepared to be unpopular.

However.

I don't think any of the women knew how bad things had become with Eddie. And that is for the best. Because they'd say things like, Bina, you have the right idea, without indicating exactly which part I had right. And honestly, I didn't want to be a disappointment to them. I am taking time in the aftermath to be truthful here and to disappoint. I hadn't the right idea. Not at all. But I'll make sure, if you read this, that by my words' end you might have it. And if you don't, keep writing and telling how you had the wrong idea to the next woman until finally we all fathom it. We'll have to write the warnings back and forth to each other. It's the only thing to do. Eventually we might even start listening and not need any more warnings.

Tomás had told me Eddie was living in Waterford
For a time.
Quite a long time.
He'd told me that with relief
Once he got sick
That his nephew, who caused all the problems in the world,
was in Waterford.
And can he help you? I'd asked that one time.
Oh God, he's no help, he said
Don't let him near me.
You wouldn't want him near you.

This was why when I received the letter from Waterford
I knew the woman had to be telling the truth
About Eddie taking advantage of her generosity.
She wrote the same words.
Don't let him near you or anyone you've any time for, she said
He is not right in the head.
If I was to reply to that woman, which I never have, I
would tell her his uncle said Eddie's father was a lovely man.
Eddie's uncle was a good friend to me and we never know
what way our children will turn out, so be mindful of that
when you are sending letters to frighten people as foolish as
yourself around the country.
Except I didn't.

Because I couldn't.
I'd only be saying, don't tell me I'm as stupid as you are,
Because I know I am.
Even though I've no intention of admitting it.

Never admit you know you're stupid
It's the surest route to feeling even more stupid.
Make out instead it was all intentional
But you've changed direction.
Just like a boat might.
Be nautical.

We'll see yet how this might sail in court.

I blame men on the radio
And politicians
Who are men on the radio.
I blame men talking about football
It's why I can't watch the television anymore
I disagree with everyone on the television
Except Theresa.
I have a free television licence
Full of people I disagree with

Eddie & I disagreed about television
Obviously.
But I will spare you that.
I have to spare you some things
But I am not for sparing you the important stuff.
And that's a warning
It took me longer than I thought to get here
But do not spare the important stuff
Do not be making your exit full of noise
Do not be making your exit with a pain in your chest
Do not be making your exit with a set of broken ears.
If possible.
Sort all those things out before you go
You want it to be a nice long sleep you'll head into.

You need to move, I told him.
Eddie grunted.
You have a week to get out. Then the locks change, I said.
A week came. He left. I thought it was over. I assumed it was finished.
It wasn't finished.
A man, that man, visited me.
In one visit I knew it wasn't finished.

The inspectors visited me. They told me what they were here for. What are you here for, I said. Come again. They repeated what they were here for. They were not here for what I assumed they'd be here for, and no, they didn't want to come in. Instead what they were here for was outside. But they might have some questions for me once they'd inspected. They used words like report, sighting, suspected, illegal and, finally, dumping.

At dumping I just laughed. Dumping I said. There's many things I can be accused of but dumping is not one of them. My first thought was it must be the Crusties. I had not given them much thought because if I were to do so they would worry me and I'd vowed not to think about where they were shitting and singing. (They'd stopped the singing between certain hours as I'd requested.)

Carry on, I said. Carry on and inspect.

Not even five minutes til they were back at my door. And me returned to the bed, now lifted again from the bed and with that lift came irritation. Help yourselves, I said. I'm asleep.

We can't get access, they said, and indicated an area up beyond my barn. I stepped out in my dressing gown and slippers and there, like they were guarding the Roman Colosseum with their scarfs across their faces, were all the Crusties stood, arms locked. Don't worry, Bina, one shouted. *No pasarán, no pasarán*, they all began chanting.

Hold on til I get my coat, I said.

●

The Crusties didn't advise Bina to let inspectors look at the land.

They didn't advise that.

●

Move aside and let them in, I instructed the Crusties, who adamant refused.

They are trespassers, the Crusties said.
They're not trespassers. They are here for the dumping.
The dumping has to be removed.
Do I look to you like a dumper? I said to them all.
They aren't here for me, they are here for the dumping.
When they come for me, there will be more of them than these fellas. A proper army or a van. Not a clipboard.

The Crusties moved beside me like bodyguards. I felt like Saddam, stood there with all this loyalty.

Carry on, I waved the inspectors through.
Go home, I said to the Crusties
I'm going back to my bed, I said.

I am an old woman who should not be disturbed in this manner. At my age, in my situation, with my dispensation, there should be some peace available to me. You're like a bunch of birds fighting and squabbling in my brain and you're making me unbalanced.

I'll be honest now, I wasn't at my best. One of the inspectors had a look about him that I had a bad feeling about because he put on a pair of blue latex gloves and removed a phone from his coat pocket & began taking photos. I stomped down the garden away from all of them and since I hadn't put on the right footwear to support such a firm stomp, I came a cropper over a chunk of something belonging to Eddie or a Crustie. Whatever took me down, hadn't I barked so often at the Crusties to leave me in peace that they did just that. Finally I had to wail. *I can't get up, I'm stuck.* And I was so tired of it all I began to cry. Phil would have been mortified. But as we all know, Phil could be wrong.

A Crustie drove me to the Accident & Emergency and I was worried they'd keep me there and then try to arrest me for whatever new thing they fancied arresting me for. My collarbone was broke, but my shoulder was not. They insisted my colour was a problem. That I was the wrong colour to go home. How is your pain, they kept asking me. I want to shoot my own head off, I said in reply.

I can report that it isn't the wisest thing to say if you are trying to go home from such a place.

That was a warning within a remarking.

Like a blanket wrapped in a quilt.

Phil said stop.

Bina stop crying.

Crying is no good to anyone and you more than anyone know it and so stop with the crying.

If you start crying, I'll start crying, she said, and neither of the two of us will be any good to the other.

That was when we ate a basket of chips with ketchup and agreed to stop all tears.

I tried to tell her another time about what I couldn't tell her, but Phil stuck to her line on old women and tears. *I've learned anytime I gave tears publicly I was soon slammed up in an uncomfortable bed other than my own*, and we both agreed that a woman's place is in her own bed.

Phil was right.

There was no room for crying unless you were on a familiar pillow.

Phil knew

What Phil knew

And that was the problem

Because I could never ascertain how much she knew.

Except the odd time she would say with no uncertainty that at our age we are already past the end and we should be facing it, Bina, and we won't face it, will we?

Then she did whisper that she admired how I was helping people face it.

I looked blank and smiled and said something about weather or water or both. If stuck, I always drew on the "W" words. I learned this from Scrabble. It's a great game for filling in the awkward pauses.

I was skittery when Phil talked this way.

I was skittery because I'd been carefully trained by the Tall Man and his rule was that those nearest and closest to us must suspect nothing and if we suspected they suspected we must immediately stop. Cease! Because you'll take everyone out and it's selfish to do that. You have been trusted and if that trust is ever blown you must stop.

All I heard was him saying stop and cease and Phil saying she admired that I was helping people.

What I should have done is asked Phil outright:
Do you know?
How much do you know?
And who has told you what you know?

But I was worried about Tomás. That without me he'd
have no one to help him and he was nearing the end and would
need me.

I was a fool.

I am not as vital or important as I thought I might be.

Tomás would have been fine.

He would have found his exit.

If I'd left him to Eddie, Eddie would have killed him.

Instead, Eddie has the two of us killed, maybe.

Bina, the Tall Man would say to me

I am warning you

Don't hesitate.

Don't hesitate with Eddie.

Kick his ass out of here.

Those were the words he said.

The exact words

Because that is his accent too.

And how, I said

Do you propose I do that?

Have you seen the size of my feet?

You haven't lost the use of your hands, he said

Change the locks.

You think locks stop a big lump like Eddie?

He'd come back in through the chimney.

If I am not to hesitate then I'll need a gun
I said.
A gun is all that will relieve me of Eddie.
That shut the Tall Man up with his prescriptions.
No talk of guns, he said, returning to Scrabble.
It reminds me of a certain place I cannot mention.
You don't need a gun, he said
You need to learn to say No.
He was right I needed to learn to say No
And not just to Eddie.
I needed to learn to say No to all men
Including him.

And the next time I found an opportunity to tell him as much
He wasn't able to hear it.
So I am going to tell him now
From here.
From where I am lying in my bed.
I am going to tell you, Tall Man
After the fact
That I was a fool not to say No to you
And not to say a proper No to Phil
Because Phil was wrong
And you were sometimes wrong.
The difference is Phil probably knew she was wrong
Whereas you never entertained any such notion.

I was chased out of my home each day by an odour

The odour's name was Eddie.

I have wondered what might have become of me if I'd never let that odour in.

We can't know now.

This is a warning:

If it smells bad, it is bad.

The Crusties were clever. I admire them now I think more on it. They sent Paul from Donegal into the hospital to me. They were cute to send him because he was a man who could sit and say nothing. He was good at looking out the window. He was good for fetching tea. He was good for delivering reports. He was good at calming me down, once he had the report delivered.

I'm not going to lie to you, Bina, but there's a bit of a situation now at the house.

What kind of a situation?

It's just all the stuff you were storing.

What storing? I'm not storing anything. Eddie has the place covered in shite but there's nothing new there.

Behind your barn. That stuff.

What stuff? I haven't been behind that barn.

Well I am sure there's an explanation then.

What have they found there?

Hospital waste, he said.

I was completely mithered. Hospital waste?! I haven't made any waste, I said. I've only been sat here 5 hours. I've only broken my collarbone. How much waste can there be? I don't even think I've used a tissue.

The texts and photos started arriving. The Kind Crustie asked me the way the Kind Crustie always did whether I wanted to see the pictures.

Don't worry, he said, we filmed it all to make sure they didn't plant anything there.

Did you know about the track back there?

Track? What track?

He revealed photos.

I didn't like what they showed

So I will spare you the details.

Needless to say I was happy not to go home from this hospital now.

Because when this hospital-waste story got out, no hospital would let me back in.

Don't worry, the Kind Crustie said.

There's bound to be an explanation.

I looked at him

He looked at me

We both knew the explanation and neither of us could say his name aloud.

I rested until the further x-rays were due. They needed to strap me to an ironing board and put me into another machine, they said. They needed to decide whether to put a bolt into my bones. I longed to have a frank conversation with them, where I expressed it would be a wasted bolt because given the shape my future was taking in the past hour I might not be sticking around.

Where did he get the waste? I asked Paul, the Kind Crustie.

I wouldn't know myself, he replied, but it was probably a criminal[43] gave it to him.

Yes, I agreed, I suppose there would be no point in stealing the stuff as it's free.

But why would he store it behind my barn? Who would want to buy it?

I think you might consider this a bit more than storage—more like a final destination.

The Lord save us, I said.

---

[43] A man had visited me. He was very unpleasant. Moody and grim. He was probably the criminal. The owner of the waste. (If he calls again, he'll not leave without taking a few bags of it with him.)

We were lucky he didn't kill the lot of us.

The Crustie didn't reply, he just stared out the window.

This was for the best

As there was nothing to be said about Eddie.

Silence was the best choice.

When finally I was let go from the hospital

Once again, I had only this Kind Crustie to rely on and bring me home.

Now Bina, the doctor said, I don't mean to press the issue, but you can't be dealing with animals or farming until the collarbone is repaired.

He looked at the Crustie.

You have to let your son handle the outdoor work or you'll be back in here to us with another break.

He is not my son, I said, emphatic.

He is a nice man, but he's not my son.

I have no sons,[44] I said

And I make no apology for it.

The doctor didn't care if I'd a son or not

But as soon as I had no son, in the social worker came

I knew this was a bad plan

Because as soon as they saw who was camping outside my back door

---

[44] I have no children at all. Just random adults who glue themselves to me.

I'd be back in here.

But I had seen where having sons could get you with Eddie

So I caved in and accepted my fate.

A health visitor would be ringing me, she said

And Meals on Wheels could be organized.

Meals on Wheels?

I'd say I'm blacklisted, was all I replied

And good enough of her she let that pass.

The Kind Crustie was in with his reassurances.

She has community support, he[45] proclaimed.

I have no such thing, I thought

I just have a gang of squatters getting under my feet and bringing me bad news.

When the Kind Crustie drove me home, he stopped.

We're getting you fed, he said.

Then you're going to sleep.

Again I had a brief glimpse that I could let this one in to use my toilet

But I clamped down on it

Because I'd been had before.

It was Phil I needed

I wanted Phil back

---

[45] The Kind Crustie was not a curious man, I admired this about him. You'll tell me anything you want me to know, he had said, and if you don't tell me it there's no need for me to ask about it.

I want her undead.

That's how it is.

Just because you can lift a box

Doesn't make you useful to me if you won't put it where I tell you to put it.

It's not useful if you put it on top of my head.

I kept waking up in a panic and thinking nonsense obvious things like that.

It had to be the drugs they'd given me.

Drugs can make you very strange.

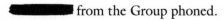

██████████ from the Group phoned.

I heard about the waste, she whirred away into the answering machine.

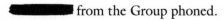

The council had slapped a dangerous-territory order on my sheds.

I told them to unslap it.

The Crusties had formed a human chain.

They were all fighting when I arrived.

I pushed my way into the middle and told them straight. I am getting into my bed and I expect quiet out here. I need to sleep. I have a broken bone and there's to be no fighting until it's fixed.

Let them in to do whatever it is they want to do, I told the swarm of Crusties. Just move all the tents closer to the door. And you, I told the officials, get on with your excavations and leave these good people alone.

There was a lot of muttering about breach of health and safety and contamination and they gave numbers for how much distance was needed to contain it. They seemed to be talking about evacuating the neighbours. Listen, I said, it's a bunch of rubbish we're talking about, not foot-and-mouth. Calm down and get on with it because the longer you stand here shouting, the more it'll contaminate wherever it sits.

I agreed all the campers and tents would move by tomorrow noon.

The Crusties insisted on a meeting.
I told them straight
No meeting until I have had a rest.
All I can say is, democracy is very noisy.
I gave in to avoid a meeting and said they must send most people away but that no more than four could stay and they could come into my kitchen until the situation resolved. But now they had to get out of my way and let me go to bed. I eyed the Kind Crustie and told him to deal with it.

This is the end of it now.

All here. All told from here is told to you from the leaba. I am back in my bed. I will not be leaving it. When was I last out of the bed? I can't remember. I have taken to the bed because a murky set of circumstances have come down around me that I cannot tell you about. God I wish I could. But it's just too risky. You understand or at least you will when you read this and you see all the rest of it (soon) splashed in the papers.

Expect the red dot very soon. Expect it any sentence. I am tired. Awful tired. I am tired of thinking of how I'll explain this all to the resisters. For my feeling now is, it is over. I will endeavour to rush through the remaining stuff I owe you or if you don't find anything here you might feel you're owed an explanation for, know that either I may not have one or I was in bed writing it and my arm may have given up on me. I could have fallen asleep. Do me a favour and close your radio ears down when all the bad talk soon[46] starts. We cannot know every reason a person has for doing a thing. Even if we think they are wrong, even if they are very wrong the way I know Phil was wrong.

I am only one woman with a biro or a pencil, depending on what falls out of the bed, and what I can or cannot reach with my bad shoulder. They'll make up lies. They'll probably

---

[46] It's going to be bad. It's going to be very bad. Phil and I will be reduced to mucky, cold headlines.

say I was dirty and demented. I was neither. I was just one-shouldered towards the end and very tired. I've decided to stay in the bed now, because anytime I get out of the bed I seem to invite a new round of trouble.

I want to quick slip in a warning here. Dear God Above Do Not Talk To The Papers. I know it's a cliché and I know no one is reading them,[47] and everyone is blaming them for everything including the football results and the weather. But they are right. DO BLAME THEM. There was an awful anorak of a man at the door and another ringing the phone. A third woman said she was a friend of my cousin. Cousin? What cousin, says I? Sure I've no cousins. I've killed them all, remember! That shut her down. But what is it here I am trying to say? It is only this. Don't talk to them. If you talk to one they start phoning from Bahrain. I have had to barricade myself in. They arrived like an army out there. And in I am now barricaded with very little food to last me. Only for the Crusties forming a ring, I'd have nothing. But I don't care, I'll go hungry before they get me for whatever it is they have now decided I've done. I can't keep up with the accusations

Stop it, the Solicitor said.
Stop what?
Stop saying you are ready to talk and phoning up the media.
I haven't touched the phone, I said. Not since.
Who's talking to the *Daily Mail* then?

---

[47] They can't close down quick enough for me. They are full of awful men called John and Andrew.

Who is this spokesperson speaking for you in the papers?
I've no clue, I said.
I'm here in bed.
I'm not talking to anyone, only myself.
And you.

I phoned the Solicitor.
It might be the lads camping out the back.
What lads?
The protestors.
Hold on til I go out and see.

The Crusties want me to know it wasn't them and it must be an enemy. Categorically not them. They said the word categorically twice. They offered to make a list of all my enemies and then apologized for getting me out of bed. They have people on the inside and their people could find out. Do no such thing, I said. I don't want to know who it is. Enemies, they repeated. This is the work of a traitor. A professional. Make a list.

The Solicitor wants me to know.
And this time I pay attention.
And tell him to send me a picture of the latest accuser.

When I see it I laugh loudly.

I am in bed when I laugh.

My shoulder hurts.

I turn over and push the envelope aside and laugh some more.

I've never set eyes on anyone in the picture he's sent.

It wakes me up. The curiosity in it. The curious element that someone is actively making rubbish up where there's no need. The world is overflowing with made-up rubbish. I've seen this since the Tall Man turned on the Tablet for me. There's so much rubbish it has made me very tired. And now there's fresh rubbish that's woken me up.

The new accusation involves a case in England. Lookit, I wasn't in England for a long time and I will tell you here and now exactly where I was when I was in England and why. I was nowhere near where they say this ███████ was assisted. I was in Loughborough briefly. I went over for work because my mother, God Rest Her, sent me. I had an awful time. I caught appendicitis over there and it didn't suit me. Eventually Mam agreed I should come back as *It wasn't right for you, Bina* was how she put it.

England wasn't for Bina.

It isn't for everyone

And it wasn't for Bina.

No matter what they're saying.

This was what Bina's mother always said of her time in England.

I left my appendix in England is all Bina will say.

I'm not going back for it.

Bina knows what she did do and what she didn't do.

Don't forget that.

That much she knows

The rest is up to yourselves.

The Solicitor wants to know what I did in England. He says he'll need evidence and proof to counter this fresh accusation.

I hear him say it on the message.

The message he leaves for me when I don't answer the phone.

I'm glad he left the message he did, though, because I have to think about who knew I was in England at all and I cannot remember if I told Eddie this. He's the most likely person to be spreading filthy untruths that will see me locked up, but since I cannot remember, this is a problem.

I have no one who might remember for me.

The other people who certainly knew I had gone to England were Tomás and Phil.

They are both gone.

They'll not be telling anyone anything to defend me.

The Crusties are right.

It's an enemy and it's time to make a list.

I'll make a list of everything I can remember and then maybe it'll come again, the parts I cannot remember. Sometimes it comes and sometimes it does not. Sometimes you're glad about that. Not everything needs to be remembered. Don't forget that when you're struggling to recall.

My mother changed the story. She changed my story and said I *had* to come back home. She said I was needed there. My siblings needed me. She forgave that money was needed and she let me come back. I am remembering that now but how much use is that in a court of law?

I have started taking small naps to help with the remembering. I am doing this because I heard a woman on the radio saying that Einstein took one-second naps to help him do difficult calculations.

It was on Raidió Na Gaeltachta.

I was amazed there I was listening to Einstein *as Gaeilge* and he helped me remember information about myself.

Would you credit it?

I'm only forgetting in English, I'm remembering in Irish.

How is that possible?

Only for Einstein.[48] [49]

I'd be blanked.

I don't like it.

The not being able to remember.

The scrambling.

---

[48] I might buy a tea towel with Einstein on it. Every time I look at it, I'll remember it was he helped me with the remembering.

[49] Forget that. No point. No tea towels needed nor allowed in prison.

It's like trying to bite something that keeps moving away from your mouth. It's like that, except the first few times you bite yourself and it hurts and then on the fourth time you stop trying. The trouble, even right here, is I can't finish the sentence because I cannot remember what you stop trying at.

This is getting very difficult

I think you can see that.

Can't you?

They are wanting me to provide information but I cannot remember any information they need me to provide.

Unfit to stand trial.

Those were four words Phil used

To reassure me.

That was Phil

Always wrong.

Unfit to stand trial, I tell the Solicitor.

Not getting out of bed, I tell the man.

Unfortunately staying in bed doesn't render you unfit to stand trial.

He cautions against it.

You're too functional, he says.

And what would you know about what way I am, I told him.

Come here and look at me and you'll see I'm unfit.

Next week, he says he'll come, but he's not hopeful.

I'll need to be dead by next week
Maybe
That's all I could think against him not being hopeful.

Now just in case there's speculation about Loughborough and what I did there . . . I will state unequivocally everything I did that would have interest to any person looking to convict me. I did a bit of cleaning work and I did factory work and finally I did some Home Help. They are going to make an awful song and dance about how many jobs I had in a short time, but there is an explanation for it and I will write it out here in as much detail as time and this excruciating shoulder pain permits.

And I think that is all it permits.

I cleaned

I worked in a factory

I was a Home Help

And then I came home, which is where I have been writing to you from ever since, and forgot about it.

And then Eddie ruined my life

And now I've gotten rid of him

And he's still ruining my life.

If I am dead and you are burying me reading this, there is to be no bad singing. D'ya hear?

I have to stop now though because of the pain.

You learn all manner of unexpected things when you lie down in bed.

My teeth are gone very painful

It's happening when I read certain words

Words with an e in them

I'm just putting this down here

In case they autopsy me

And could find out the cause.

I won't be able to go to the dentist again.

I'm not moving

And dentists don't come into the bed to you.

I can't go anywhere when my teeth are this bad

It even hurts to turn my head

It even hurts to have a head

They just throb and throb and throb.

On account of my teeth, I have to phone ███████ [50]

Could you bring me painkillers?

What's wrong, she said.

It's my teeth, I said. I can't walk.

I had to say I can't walk because otherwise why would she bring them?

You need to go the dentist, she said

Oh it's not that kinda thing, I said.

---

[50] There is no Phil to phone anymore. It was always Phil I phoned.

I won't last long, I thought.

It'd be a waste of his time to be drilling.

David Bowie came back. He talks to me of exhaustion and blandness. It might be a hint. Escape, Bina! Bowie says. Get out. Find out who you are! Another time he recommends I watch a film with a man called Stanley in it. Ah I'm not much for television, Mr. Bowie, I said. It's a film, Bina, says Bowie. It would be a nice day out for you to go and see it. Put on a scarf though, and keep your ears warm.

Sure I'm warm here in me bed, I said.

I'll stop bothering you, said he.

Oh you're no bother. You're no bother at all. But he was gone before I completed my second delivery of the word bother.

David Bowie came back.[51] He didn't abandon me. He came back to talk about Lou Reed and Iggy Pop. I'm not good with names anymore, I told him. Mr. Bowie says he'll sing me

---

[51] He was very like my teeth. They would hurt for three days in a row, then stop. Mr. Bowie would visit three times in the one week, then I'd never know if he'd reappear. He was a great distraction to the shoulder and the teeth.

a song. Then he says he'll sing me a song every day. Oh there's no need for that, I wave the back of my hand at him. He's on a chair with his back against the wall. Watch your back, I said, I think that wall is damp. I don't invite him into my bed because it would be very bad manners and we'd be squished. Also, he's smoking and he might set the house on fire if he drops ash on my bed and then where would I be? I might be in a better place though, if I go up in smoke with David Bowie.

He leans forward on the stool and sings to me while he smokes and thinks.

It's a new song he sings. Although I'll be honest, I'm not fluent in his songs. He could be singing me anything and I wouldn't mind a bit. And then he's gone again.

He only came back one more time. Do you know what I'm good at, Bina? What's that, Mr. Bowie? Synthezising and refracting how we live. Oh you are, I agreed. I'll be honest, I didn't understand what he meant. You're helping me live with your visits, I told him. He smiled and drifted off again, thinking and humming. He was wearing small round sunglasses which I found a bit distracting because I could see my reflection in them and I looked a state—but what woman has time to prepare for these visits?—and if I prepared he'd never come and if I thought about the visits I wouldn't let him in because of all the warnings I've already given you here. In = Din. I'll add an exception. Unless it's David Bowie and he's sat on a stool humming. I might warn you not to let him smoke since the place does smell of cigarettes after he leaves and it's not the best smell to be sniffing when you are laid up the way I am.

I lay in my bed, listening.

The radio told me who had died and where I could find them reposing and the exact time they'd cease reposing and go into the ground. Another voice complained about the lack of public toilets in our towns. Lack of toilets causes distress for many, she said. Parking charges should cover public toilets. Another caller phoned to say there should be no parking charges. It was a disgrace and he'd be happy use his own toilet, thanks, if parking were free.

We don't know what real charity means in this country, came another caller, unrelated to the public toilets. The conversation was disrupted by *Went to a River with My Fishing Rod But I Couldn't Even Find a Spot to Cast My Line Because of All the Bushes*—confused fella phoning that there were too many bushes in this country.

I needed the right tractor for the right job. Or so an advert sung out stridently to me.

We Are No Longer in a Democracy We Are Living in a Dictatorship gave me another 20 minutes of opining about smoking. I was taking it all in. Just allowing it to go into my ears and swish about my brain, unimpeded. I wasn't going to be thinking any more important thoughts. I would let others occupy my thinking vessel. They could have it. It was empty. It was at this point I realized people have no problems at all, they have nothing bothering them if bushes and fishing are the worst of it.

A woman phoned the radio on Friday and said people were having their sex against the gable of her house and it was interrupting her night's sleep. I want them to go elsewhere, she said. They are even out there in the rain. Yowling. Like a bag of cats.

And what had she tried to deter them with?

A bucket of soapy water, she said.

And did it work?

It did not, she said, there's even more of them out there now.

Are they reproducing, somebody texted in.

Another caller suggested a hose. A fire hose. Soapy water was too good for them. She needed a water cannon, he espoused.

I admired the woman with the soapy bucket. They only gave her first name and the area where she lived. I wrote down her name in case I was ever passing it.

I revised my thoughts. I was wrong.

Some people were being plain tormented.

●

Bina wonders about Phil's point of view
She concludes Phil thought she was a burden.
Or about to become one
So she removed herself.

She was no burden, thinks Bina
She was no burden at all

●

One time recent somebody shouted at me in the street.

Baby killer! he roared, waving his arm and fingers fiercely at my face.

If you don't get outta my way, you'll be the first baby I kill, I told him.

Stern and firm, and off he hoofed.

Phil didn't do enough shouting

That was her problem.

She requested, like a sane person would

And when she found no permission

She removed herself.

I have too many versions of Phil now

And that's my problem

I just want her back

The best version.

She and I,

Giving out

And

Lively.

█████████ from the Group phoned and said she'd heard Eddie was coming home to testify against me.

She said something about a plea bargain.

I asked her how she was.

This was to avoid telling her to stop watching American crime shows.

That we don't live in plea bargains.

We live in Ireland.

Where it takes a century to get to court & rapists and murderers[52] are acquitted and old women like me won't ever get a fair trial.

She was so surprised I asked how she was that she said she was in a hurry and had to go.

I didn't believe her.

She didn't expect me to ask her how she was.

This is what we've become.

See.

She expects me to billow on about my anxieties about what Eddie will and won't say.

She doesn't expect I want to know how she is.

Because we do not want to know how the other is

---

[52] Or they get the sort of sentences more appropriate for stealing a bag of frozen peas.

We want only to talk and hear tell of ourselves.
Since I lay down in the bed I lost all interest in myself.
You should all try it.
It is very peaceful.

It is a few days before I thought again on what she'd told me.
It took a few days for it to fully register.
Eddie was coming back.
They were going to use Eddie against me.
I would have to phone the Solicitor.
He would be even less hopeful now.

The thing is, if that fella can testify against me then I will
have to go to court
Because I will have to testify as to what I have put up with
from Eddie.
He's not indicted, the Solicitor said.
He's not the problem here.
Indict him, I said, and hung up.

You have to stop hanging up on me, the Solicitor said
when he phoned me back.
I can't stop, I said.

What more proof is there I am not fit to stand trial if I can't stop hanging up on the man who's to defend me.

Just stop doing it, he said.

I was fed up of men telling me to stop doing things when they never heeded me asking them to stop starting things. If he wanted me to stop hanging up on him, he could start by stopping phoning me and he could come over here and see for himself that it's Eddie I need defending against and not the other way around. And I never did anything for anybody that wasn't asked of me. And we have, nearly, all the videos to prove it.

Nearly.

Except Phil's.

Who was wrong.

Left a silly misleading note

When I was on my way over there to help her by persuading her she didn't need to be dead.

No matter what she said about the baking and about the claw, not being able to bake is not a good enough reason for being dead. We all know that. Even Eddie, thick as a brick, knows it.

I was going over there to tell Phil she could move in with me or I would move in with her and then she wouldn't need to bake. She could have her claw hand and she wouldn't need to do anything. Neither would I. I could lie down here the way I am lying down now and writing to you. And when she shouted for help I could get up and go to her and help her because she was Phil, and we had known each other for a very long time and there's nothing I wouldn't do for her, but the big problem is I forgot to tell her this. And this is the problem with forgetting, and this is where the doctor has misunderstood me.

I have started to worry about what Eddie's going to say about me in the courts.

And I have no Phil to go over and discuss it with.

And this is the worst of Phil being gone.

It was only Phil who understood how ridiculous Eddie was.

It was Phil I confided in the most

And now Phil's gone.

Phil should be testifying against Eddie. I know she would. I know this because she once said to me during a very difficult conversation, after he had been shouting at me, *if you kill him, I'll defend you.*

You're joking, I said.

I am not, she replied.

It would be a mercy killing and it would be a great public service.

How would it be a mercy killing?

He is unmerciful. Relentless, she said, and if he did it himself the rope would probably snap. So if you do it, for me it's a precaution.

I was stern with her.

You shouldn't joke about that, I said. Mercy killing isn't for joking.

Give over, she replied.

We drank another cup of tea and she let it out of her.

When you think about it, isn't it a miracle he hasn't been shot? Might happen yet, she said. He's on target for getting shot I'd say. If you can hold out and be patient.

I agreed with her, but it was terrible advice. If you are reading this and you are locked in with an Eddie or tolerating a nasty man or woman—don't. Don't wait for anything.

Get gone

By whatever means necessary.

No one will come for you

And no one will save you from them.

This much I know.

Imagine the very worst and then see it happening and use the sight of it to flee.

A warning.

I have had some of my finest thoughts lying down.

I have experienced the glorious mind, as it was described by that woman on the radio while I was lying down.

She was an American and I've knocked my knees together in frustration while lying here that I never wrote down her name. Not even her initial. It might have been Mary. It might have been Madeleine. She spoke like a woman who had a great brain insulated by a good, warm curl of hair. She was a very solid woman. But since I have no name for her and I have no surname for her, I have instead created a head and good crop of hair for her. I have imagined that brain of hers, as she instructed us—and it wasn't instructing she was at: it was remarking. I caught my remarking from her. I was always remarking to myself, but now I'm doing my remarking in a more formal capacity for yourselves, and for after I'm gone, and I am very glad of it. For it has been a long life of being talked at, often unintelligently, and at this late hour in the departure lounge of life, I am happy to do the full remarking aloud and down onto these papers. Ordinary extraordinary remarking was what the woman on the radio was at, but she caught me when she told of how people were chased by that which was catching up to them and it was on hearing that that she gave me the final permission to lay still. To lie there and experience the glory of my own mind, for hadn't I been long chased daily from my house by the intolerable agony of Eddie wrecking my inglorious head? I came to understand that what I had been doing in the Group was affording people the very same right. That is, the right to lie still.

I might say to you that if you are availing of the same right while reading this, that would be grand. That would be very fine indeed. If you might be lying down and exploring the glory of your own mind. You'll find no judge in me. I won't be snipping at your heels telling you the washing up is waiting and the net curtains need a wash and you should be eating more than three carrots and a slice of bread.

I'd tell you look up at the ceiling and enjoy it.

The difference with this woman and what I liked about her was that she wasn't interested in taking over my mind or your mind. She didn't want to occupy it. She'd no interest in telling me what to think or that she was right and her right was the only right and all else was left. Left out in the rain and rumble and be damned and be shut of it. Not at all. She was only interested in letting her own mind be fortified and plentified and to be doing its exercise. She wanted her brain to squeeze itself joyously out.

Resignation is not acceptance.

I think that was what the glorious-mind woman said on the radio.

But if she didn't say it there

Well, I am saying it here.

Women who leave, Phil said. What do you think of them?

I was gearing up to answer her question. Had inhaled breath to commence when she changed it.

I mean women who don't leave, what do you think of them?

I think of them the way I think of any woman, I replied.

I hadn't answered her question.

Phil wouldn't let me away with that.

I could rely on her to come back.

Come again, she said, you haven't answered my question.

Women who don't leave, what do you think of them?

Do you mean like myself?

I do, she said. And I'm also talking about myself. I never left. Not properly.

Ah but you figured out how to have a bit of fun.

We'll say no more on that, she said.

I think women who don't leave are very stupid. I think many probably kill themselves in the process and I don't judge any woman for it because sometimes it is hard to see which way the door opens even when you're looking at it.

And what about you, I asked her. What do you think of it?

Me, she said. I don't know what I think about it at all. That's why I am asking you.

With hindsight Phil could be very unhelpful with these kinds of questions and I expect that's why she thought it was just fine to leave that note on the kitchen table.

I do talk to her, you know.

Maybe that's why I lie down.

Now

To talk to Phil.

We'll see.

Soon.

If I don't get up again

We'll know

Then

That is why.

That may not have been the same for the Tall Man. I am going to think about that while I am lying here and I'll let you know.

These are some of the questions I am going to think on.

Did the Tall Man try to tell people what to do?

Did the Tall Man ever tell me what to do?

What would the Tall Man make of what I am now doing?

Why am I even questioning the Tall Man, when I know full well he did an awful lot of good?

Was it Phil being wrong that made me question the Tall Man?

Should I instead be questioning Phil?

Is it Phil these questions are for?

And now I am back to the start again, because before I can think about the questions I have to figure out who I am questioning. To do that it appears I need to lie here, be still and maybe even sleep on it. That isn't a question, in case I am confusing you. That is a remarking.

And I will say this of the woman with the great head of hair and the brain on the boil, I would say she relieved me of every ounce of anything bad or any trace of guilt I had that we in the Group helped people carry out their choices about ▬▬▬▬. At least, she relieved me of it until Phil went and did what she did. And Phil was wrong. I cannot accept Phil's choice. I cannot accept Phil's choice even though I have accepted every other stranger's choice. I cannot accept it and perhaps the flaw is my own. But accept it, I will not.

Always write down the name of the person saying intelligent things or who is relieving your burdens on the radio. This is a warning. Not a remarking. You'll need the name later, maybe. Write it down.

I want Phil undead.
It's as simple as that
Phil was wrong
I had no idea how wrong

And now I have.
And I want her back
Undead
Now.

I want her on the phone
I want Phil in my ear
Being bossy.
Oh, she could be bossy when she was well
Telling me the things she told me
Harassing me over there to help her
I want her back so I can tell her
What I was on my way to tell her
The day she was took
Or the day she took
Herself
By herself.
I was going over there to tell her
She was wrong
And I had no intention of helping her
Do to herself what was wrong
To be doing.
I knew she was wrong
And I failed to show her she was.
And that's a fact.

She disarmed me
By talking

She disarmed me
Because she talked.
She talked about what she wanted
When none of us talked about what we wanted
Which was her
Undead.
Alive.
Back here.
Now.
Life's all wrong
With no Phil.

It's how it is and how it will be, until we too are all dead
and are, maybe, with the help of God, able to tell her straight
into the eyes: Phil, you were wrong, there was no need for you
to go, your time wasn't up, not even a bit up, only momen-
tarily appearing to be up, but we could have sorted it. Oh, we
could have had that sorted.

Sorted? I can hear her reply. Would you give over? Be quiet.
Shut up, you, I'm napping. Take the top bunk there. Are you
cold? Take the extra blanket off my feet.

She'd give you everything, Phil. Except the thing you
want now, which is herself.

Here.

(Still.)

Alive.

Undead.

The Tall Man said he always asked the same first question.

I have a first question, he said.

Every time.

Why do you want your life to end?

If, the Tall Man said, they don't tell me they can no longer do the things they used to do and the things that gave them pleasure then I won't help them. He stretched his back in the chair when he said *don't*.

What if they tell you they can't do things that they never previously mentioned or never previously did?

He paused.

They've never said that. He placed a blank tile on the Scrabble board.

Well, how would you know what they could or did do, if you hadn't known them for years?

I trust people to tell me the truth, he replied.

I don't want to help anyone not needing nor asking for my help. We are not out actively recruiting. They come for us, it's not the reverse.

He was right.

I nodded.

But he didn't know Phil.

This was the difference.

He wouldn't know the way I do that Phil was wrong. That when Phil said she couldn't bake anymore, he wouldn't know that Phil was terrible at baking and was being denied nothing by not being able to bake. She didn't even like baking. She should have been stopped from baking in the interests of the fire brigade.

But somehow looking at that blank tile

There didn't seem much point

In talking about a dead woman

Who couldn't bake

And who was awful at baking.

I swapped an e back into the tile pouch.

I had four e's.

You always get the e, he observed.

Bee, seem, unseen, he muttered. Before catching himself and shutting up. He was giving me clues. He had warned us all about the dangers of clues. *You know nothing. You hint at nothing and you leave with nothing and leave nothing behind you,* he'd said when he gave me the envelope with the first address I was to visit, before adding, *you'll say nothing* and *as far as you're concerned you're at nothing and all will be well.*

He said all will be well as though he'd read it in a greeting card.

Like he didn't actually believe it.

At all.

And like he'd said it a hundred times and never believed it and walked out the door every single time not believing it, but relieved he'd gotten away with it.

Stop roundabouting it, Bina.

That's me

To myself.

I'm roundabouting again, amn't I.

Need to keep straight.

Not be dizzy in circles.

Need to tell it straight

Have to find a way to tell it all, with or without me in it.

Keep it straight, Bina

Or you'll confuse them.

That's what the Solicitor keeps telling me too.

Not unlike the Tall Man, the Solicitor says answer only the question you're asked.

Not more, nothing less.

Am I in the way?

I'm only in the way.

This wasn't unusual heard. It wasn't unusual to hear it. You could *not at all* it. You could *not at all* them. But you couldn't eradicate the thought of it. You couldn't get at the part of them that had started to feel it or had maybe felt it all their lives. You wouldn't even know what someone felt all their lives and whether it was now or then they were feeling it and when was then and how was now? Maybe they could barely arrive at now because of then.

You could only go in, deliver the meal or give them a lift and the signal that someone cared that they carried on, at least long enough that the dinner wasn't wasted. Even if you didn't care. Even if you'd never cared. Even if you couldn't care less.

Even if it was raining, your feet were wet & you wondered whatever possessed you to volunteer for Meals on Wheels in the first place when you'd have been happier in your own bed.

What often struck me going in with Meals on Wheels was this. First, I was useful. I like to be useful. Second, because I was coming in, they felt they were going out. But it was never going to be clear why and what I was bringing in with me.

I've gotten awful down on the Tall Man
Lately
I don't know why this is.
I think it's because I am here
And he's there
Wherever there is
And we haven't heard a word from him.

That's not unexpected.

He warned me about that.

If anything goes down, don't expect to hear from me ever again.

I will disappear. I will have to.

He laid down his single planks.

Do you know how many years I'd serve?

His eyes said life.

You should plan to do likewise, he said.

And where would I disappear to?

That's the great thing about disappearing, he said. No one will know in advance. Not even you.

So

Don't ever need to disappear, he said.

It's very complicated, disappearing.

There are two outcomes.

One, they catch you or two, you make yourself uncatchable.

He meant dead.

Why didn't he say dead?

These were the conversations where he started to trouble me

When he spoke in roundabout language

The way I have started talking in roundabout language.

But roundabouting is no good to anyone.

Is it?

I prefer emphatic

And in lying down there's no roundabouting
It's emphatic.
I'm going no place and you'll have to come for me.
Come and find me.

Was Eddie emphatic?
Or was he just bone- and boom-headed?
Eddie was a lump
A lump isn't emphatic.
A lump is an excuse for whatever is underneath it.
We investigate lumps.
It's an error.
We should emphatically not investigate them when the
excuse beneath them is a whole human.

You know what brings people down in the end?
This was the Tall Man as he was about to play his turn.
And then he played it.
His word?
Empathy.

Don't get involved
And don't give out too much information
That will have you involved.
Another thing, the Tall Man said.
Once you are involved
Very hard to be uninvolved.

He used to annoy me with these snippets.

Because he was reminding me that the error of involvement was snoring in my spare bedroom.

His comments only turned the snores up louder

And had them ricochet around the place howling, laughing at me.

And me, I'd be roundabouting to myself that I'd only taken Eddie in because otherwise he would have unloaded himself onto Tomás, who might never reach for the alarm or alert again. He would have been unfathomably trapped in a way that I was not. I could still open my back door and leave daily. Tomás was stuck in the bed.

Were you ever involved? I asked him.

If I told you that, I'd be giving out information, the Tall Man said.

And if I give you information, you might find yourself passing it to another.

And on it would go

And that's how people fall.

He said.

I don't intend to fall.

The next day I heard he'd left suddenly.

The Group were talking about it.

The Group were phoning and asking each other if anyone had seen him.

The Group were puzzled.

I wasn't puzzled.

I had begun to see exactly what this man was about.

I was unsure if I liked it or I disliked it

I was sure a part of it troubled me.

But here I am.

And there he is.

I'm wrong

And a curse upon him that I have to admit it

But he was right.

Nothing further to be said

If you don't heed the warnings

███████ from the Group phoned.

Have you heard anything? she said.

Not a word, I said.

It's not right, she said.

What are you expecting? I said.

That he'll come out waving a big sign about where he is so they can lock him up?

Yes, she said.

Well, you're very foolish, I said.

Then I felt foolish because here was she phoning me and she on trial for nothing and me . . .

Well.

We need to talk about the mess you're in, ███████ said.

There's nothing to say.

Nothing to be said about it at all.

And now I can see that this ████████ is probably the Mole.

She is likely the Mole if there is a mole in this casserole

If she ever phones again

I should probably go ahead and ask her

Are you the Mole, ██████?

✉

Does it matter who the Mole is?

Does it?

I think that was a warning.

Or maybe a remarking

I think it doesn't matter who the Mole is

Just expect there is one and then you won't be a bit surprised.

Does it matter whether it's a warning or a remarking at this stage?

Would warnings prevent remarking?

I have no idea.

That's up to ye.

I'm in here

You're out there.

That's where we are

Now.

This is where it's at.

Right?

Have I that part right?

I don't know if I'm lying down too long and it has all gone
to my head.

The problem is you can't answer me, so I've to answer for
you.

I should have figured ▇▇▇▇▇▇▇ was the Mole on account
of what she said about my curtains.

I think you can do better than those curtains, she said.
They don't do much for the place.

That's a suspicious thing to say, isn't it, when you're only
calling in to drop off a plastic bag.

How can you wade so handily into the territory of how
someone's curtains should be?

Unless you are bringing them new curtains, that is

Inside that plastic bag

Then you lay into them.

I asked Phil about the curtains.

You're overthinking it, she said.

It's not like you to overthink things, Bina.

You're right, I said.

Has Forty Guts been insulting your curtains?

Probably. But it was a woman who said something that set me off.

A woman?

Yes.

And did you know this woman?

Not very well.

Well now, why would you let a woman you barely know into your kitchen to insult your curtains and then actually listen to her?

You're right, I said

I am, Phil replied. Sure I'm always right.

Phil was wrong.

She was wrong about the other

But she was right about the curtains

And I see now she's probably letting me know from wherever it is she has landed up in the next life that the curtain cribber was the Mole.

Once Phil said casually
You have Eddie.

I nearly exploded.

I'm only codding you, she smiled.

I know he's nothing but a trial. I'd rather be on trial for his murder, I said

Oh you would, she agreed. I'd join in.

Now I am on trial for the one I didn't do
Instead of him
The only one I should have done.

One of the things the families sometimes say is they wish they'd known.

That is the only time I am stuck.

They'll say they wish they knew more.

What more is there to know if your loved one wants to be gone and doesn't want to tell you?

I thought that until I discovered Phil was wrong.

I wanted very badly for a note or a letter.

A letter that told me why she went ahead and changed the plan.

I was angry with her for changing the plan

I had the right plan

Her revised plan was the wrong one.

And I really wished she hadn't used that red baling twine to make it all look different.

It only created even more suspicion.

They searched the place here high and low trying to find a match for it. Of course they found none because it was Phil who was wrong, not me.

But the searching threw up things that made them awful excited, and when people are excited they start digging, and that's a state of affairs you should always avoid.

Even if they find nothing.

Nothing can become something.

Think about that

Ever seen them stop a man in the street or a woman in the shop?

As soon as they say Stop

It is automatically something

It's automatically everyone looking

Everyone knowing it's something

Automatically everyone asking, everyone knowing what is the something.

And the man or woman who doesn't know will always reply with something

And the something is speculating.
And speculating isn't a good thing
I seen that.

Did you ever see a man on a bike clicking his fingers like
he is singing a song in his head?
Well, never doubt he's not singing a song.
Because whether he is singing a song or not
Look long enough and he'll start singing one for you.

If they are looking
They'll find something.
If they are looking and they want to find something
They'll find a way that something is found.
There are ways and means. It's the way of the determined.

Can you fault them?
I can
But can you?

•

If they'd asked Bina what she did
She might have told them
Except they didn't ask
They assumed.
Looked only to back up the assumptions.
She wasn't unaccustomed
She knew there wasn't much point in fighting assumption.
She had seen where resistance/that insistence had gotten her.

•

Phil was wrong.

She didn't want to implicate me, but she wouldn't let me help her.

Now Eddie is gone

I can finally focus on Phil

And why she was wrong.

Here and Now.

Phil wasn't always wrong. You see, the thing you need to know is I've known Phil a long time. I don't like what they are saying about her now she's gone. She knew what she wanted and they're all missing that. They don't know what she wanted because they never asked her. I hope they'll ask me in the court. I hope they call me Mrs. and ask me what Phil wanted. I'll tell them. But they don't listen to women in the courts. We know that.

Phil and I had our deaths and our disagreements. We had our tears. We had our phone calls and we ate a lot of pie over many years. I like to look at a pie. I like to admire a pie. Phil liked to eat it. And that may be why she got the diabetes. She said it was very unfair she got the diabetes and I cannot disagree with her there. Diabetes is very unfair.

Once we had a very strong disagreement, but I am not going to tell you about it because it's not fair to tell about disagreements with friends once they are dead. You keep those things close. You don't blab about them. We both cried, and I was surprised at that. That two women can make each other cry that way. Phil said it was nothing but a misunderstanding and we were over it now. We ate a basket of chips with ketchup in a pub to recover. We'll have a cup of coffee,[53] Phil said. We're over it. Me, I kept on crying. Bina, she said, you're always crying. To be honest, it hurt my feelings and I never cried much since. Never cried official-like.

And if it's over for me with the court case, I will not cry. I won't cry because Phil wouldn't like that. It's embarrassing when old women cry, she'd say. We weren't old women when we cried though. She only said that since we became old women.

---

[53] We didn't trust the tea in that pub.

How much Phil knew
Bina doesn't know
What she knew
If she knew
But now Bina can see what families mean when they say
they wished they'd known more, or that they wish there was
more to know.

One thing about families though
Sometimes they don't want to know.
They say they do.
You tell them
And they lose the brain on you
Call you bad words.
Evil deeds.

That's what happened when I told
Phil's daughters the truth
About their mam.
Our mam, they'd say
All possessive-like.
Your mam, I'd think, yes.
But my friend.
My good friend Phil was wrong.

How much did Phil know?
I don't know
What she knew
If she knew.
Or how she could have known.
But enough was said, the way these things are said and
don't need explaining between friends.
Unlike the way things have to be spelled out for families.
The difference between friends and family.
I can know Phil was wrong and I don't have to prove she
wasn't.

I can know Phil was right and I don't have to prove she was.
I can just know Phil
For who Phil was.
Wrong or right
Or both
And the bits between
Until she's dead.
And then I go the bizarre way of the family up in my head,
wanting to know who and how and did and what and why and
if and wrong, wrong, wrong.

I wish I had known what Phil knew. And when exactly she
knew it.

The problem is the daughters.
They don't think Phil was wrong
They think I am wrong about Phil being wrong.
I am wrong about many things.
Many, many things.
But I'm not wrong about Phil.

They think I killed her.
I never killed her
Not at all.

Sure how could I kill her if I was on my way over there to
tell her, *you're wrong Phil, you're wrong.*
Don't open the bag with the glass in it.
Just stay there in your chair til I put the kettle on for the
pair of us.

It was the final cups of tea with Tomás that had me convinced of the power of the pot. That every person could make
the right decision if only the cup was properly brewed, and
until the cup of tea was brewed proper they wouldn't be as
clear as a person should be if they have a decision to make.
That was a warning.
If you are not clear
Or if the cup doesn't taste quite right
Don't make any decision until it does.
Sometimes the taste may be the right one, but you're still
not clear.
Very good. Empty the cup. Lie down and wait. Be still,
stop thinking, and your decision will be made only when it's
ready to be made.

•

How can Bina be so sure Phil was wrong?

Well, that was the one good thing about Eddie

Any woman ever exposed to him will have the correct barometer of when enough is enough.

We have asked Bina about this.

We asked her the question.

How, Bina, did you know Eddie had to go?

•

Go on and ask me that question:
How, Bina, did you know when you'd had enough?
And that Eddie had to go.

I knew because I felt more sick than usual in my own house that week, and I did not like the man who came looking for Eddie that time.

I had suspected Eddie could do me in

I had not suspected Eddie would be happy to have me kidnapped by international criminals and money men over a bag of pills.

There's been an awful lot of confusion about the pills.
They were Eddie's pills.
Not my pills.

Eddie said I made it all up.

That no man visited me

That there was no bag of pills.

You're making that up to get rid of me.

But I'd enough reason to get rid of him

Before that creep paid his visit.

Looking for Eddie.

Is he here?

Head in the door scanning about.

He's not.

When will he be back?

I've no clue.

Head looking around, scanning the place.

If you want to kill him, I said

That'd be grand.

He didn't like that suggestion.

He seemed angry.

I'm only joking, I said. There's no useful meat on him anyway, only whale blubber.

For weeks I watched the post. I was convinced Phil would have sent me a postcard to say goodbye. I even imagined what kind of a postcard. But the postcard never came. Only the Guards came. Again and again, with more questions. Persistent questions. Eddie didn't help.

Eddie wasn't helpful.

The Guards are here again!

He enjoyed it.

Offered to make them tea.

Come in lads, you're very welcome.

He was clearing me out

You see.

That had become his plan

And here were the men to help him deliver it.

They asked Eddie if they could search the cupboards.

They asked Eddie if they could search the cupboards without a warrant.

Work away, Eddie said, acting like he owned the place.

You'll do no such thing, I protested, without a warrant.

What are you hiding in them, Eddie laughed boldly.

The Tall Man warned me that if they came and searched, they needed a warrant. I don't know how he knew this. Had he been searched? I didn't know this until he told me. I am warning you: If they come and search they need a warrant.

The Tall Man gave me a paper that told me certain things. Because I never throw anything away I can be near certain the paper is in a cupboard.

We can get a warrant, the Guard said

We can get a warrant if we want to.

Good, I said.

Come back when you have one.

They said they didn't need any warrant to ask me questions.

I answered each question with *no comment*.

Til the questions stopped.

Every question I didn't answer

Eddie supplied information.

I forget the information.

In fairness to the Guards, they did say firmly

It was me they were interviewing and if they had questions for him they'd address him.

Eddie didn't like that.

I knew he'd punish me for it.

It wasn't the first time they came looking for me.

They came after Tomás

But I was ready.

I had listened to the Tall Man carefully.

That one was no problem.

Tomás was dead and he had, I would later come to conclude, sent the Tall Man to me.

With Tomás

The questions were simple.

You delivered him Meals on Wheels. Was there anything unusual? Out of place? Did he seem different?

I knew very little about the man. He seemed weaker and I know the Home Help was aware of his condition. Maybe you should ask her? I went in and said a few hellos and I collected 5 euros and was on my way because he was not the last on my list.

I have to do a big loop you know, I said. There were people waiting on me and their food would be cold if I dallied.

Was the fire on or off?

I have no recollection of the fire, I said. I put down the food tray and I barely had time to say much to him.

And could I provide an alibi for where I was at this time?

Indeed I can. I was with Phil. You can go over and ask her.

Had you any specific reason for visiting her?

Yes, I said. I did. She's my friend.

I let a pause pass between did and friend. The Tall Man had taught me the power in a pause. They'll follow the pause to nowhere, he said. If you act suspicious they'll follow that. Give them a lot of empty pointless pauses to nowhere, and if you are lost just remember that first question I ask everyone.

Again, they asked this question when they came about Phil.

Again, I answered the same way.

She was my friend, I said. There wasn't a day I wouldn't be in touch with that woman. Check your records.

They got the warrant alright.

But I found the paper.

I burnt it.

I burned many papers.

Eddie probably told them.

Arrested under the suspicion of assisting something or other (and attempting to interfere with a corpse).

What? I said.

Don't be ridiculous.

I went to visit a woman for a cup of tea. I did not go over there to interfere with a corpse. She was a woman the last time I visited her.

And when was that?

The day before, I said. The way I visited or spoke with her every day. She had eyelids that were flapping up and down. She was in good spirits. She was Phil, I said. She was no corpse.

I was very upset when they asked me the trick questions. The Tall Man had warned me, they ask you the trick questions to get you emotional. Then they stare at your eyeballs and look for clues. Don't blink! He was emphatic. Do not look left. Ever. Or they'll know you are lying. I was puzzled. Why would looking left mean you are lying? He admitted he'd learned this from reading an interview with a passport-control officer in the newspaper and had no idea exactly why it meant that, but do not look left, ever. I imagine a lot of people get run over from following that part of his advice.

Phil, of course, had not burned her papers.

Because Phil hadn't been trained by the Tall Man.

Phil, in contrast and all foolishness, had written out a series of instructions on the kitchen table. She had written a bogus letter to me telling me she was going to be away for a while & thanking me for the lend of the glass.

She rang the alarm bell of suspicion without me even trying.

I did wonder
Why
Why she did this?

We are waiting for the Coroner's report.
We'll see what's in the report
And the toxicology tests.
They take a lifetime.
You could be resurrected before they figure out what killed you.

After I left Tomás
I went to Phil's house
I'd never done that before
I've never had to do it since.

The Tall Man had warned me not to do that.
I didn't listen
Because sometimes I don't listen.
I didn't listen to the Tall Man.
I was too upset about Tomás.
That's not unreasonable.
Is it?

✉

Show me the woman who is not upset by suffering?
And I'll accept I am unreasonable.

✉

██████████ phoned
I think you have the glass.
What glass?
The glass.
Oh, the Glass.
Yes.
There's only one glass.
Well, we need to keep the Glass circulating
The Glass must not remain.
Oh, that's right
Not remain.
Is there anything else?
No
Just the Glass.
OK
Just the Glass so.

The Glass was one of the troubles. I had moved the Glass to Phil's by accident. The Glass was wrapped in a plastic bag. A Spar bag. Inside the bag were a pair of latex gloves that the wearer put on before taking the Glass out of the bag. Once on, the Glass could be removed. I need to recall how the Glass ended up at Phil's. I think I had left it in the car. And the Tall Man taught me to be very, very careful about leaving things in cars.

In Ireland they'd steal a person out of the front seat of a car, but where he lived there was less trouble with thieving. He warned me hard. Never leave ANYTHING in the car. The car is how they catch you.

Repeat

Never leave anything in the car.

Don't blink. Look left. Or leave anything in a car.

The hymn-structions were mounting.

He trained me so carefully. He might have over-trained me. I was visiting Phil, and took the bag into her house and left it on her table when I sat down. She had me come into the living room and we were absorbed in something, I don't recall what.

The next I knew, she phoned.

I washed your glass, she said

It was sweating mad inside that bag.

What are the gloves & the syringe for?

Oh, nothing at all.

They were just in the bag.

Oh good, she said, I nearly threw them in the fire.

They're here, she said. Will I rinse the syringe?

No, no I said. Leave it in the bag.

What's inside the Glass is for you, when you decide you need it, I said.

I thought as much, she said. I put it in the breadbin. You're very good.

I'll need the glass back, though, I said. I didn't mean to leave it.

I knew the Tall Man would take a Tall Man's view on me forgetting the Glass. He had trained me the way you'd train a spy or a soldier. I enjoyed the training. It was like we were on a mission. He even took me out into the woods to practise. We didn't go far. Down to the lake, parked, found a clump of trees and he said, follow me. He trained me out there in what he was calling safe operational and conscious tactics.[54] Be aware of your surroundings, he told me. Turn your head

---

[54] Scampering around, bending up and down uncomfortably in the mud and falling over would be a better description.

around you. He made me sit in an uncomfortable position squatting and watch a bird in the distance. He said it was very dangerous and that people could not ever be discovered or caught or find themselves set up doing what we were doing. We've to be very aware, he said. We've to be ahead. We've to imagine the worst because we are relieving the worst, and those who are requesting relief will be returned to the worst should we fail them. We don't fail, he said. We cannot afford to. Unless they change their minds, which is fine. What then? You leave, he said. Oh right. Of course. He looked aggrieved, like I should have known the answer. I was new at it. I barely knew the questions.

The Tall Man enunciated carefully. His language was the language of justification and defence. He was smart this way. He wouldn't necessarily argue with you, because he wouldn't need to. He explained to me his technique. He explained this was why he played so much Scrabble. Think about it, he said. Think about how words sit beside each other, think about how one word can blend and become another. Become aware of the shape of the words leaving your mouth. Be non-committal in all that you say. We are using the language of cover. We have to cover. We have to protect. We have to honour the wishes of our clients.

I had no good clue what he was wittering on about, so I covered and nodded.

I had a feeling that once I got out of this uncomfortable squat and staring at this bird who held no interest for me, I would then understand his take and his tone, and if I didn't I would at least finally be back indoors in the warm. In the meantime, it was exciting to be away from Eddie for any purpose whatsoever. Except, in the meantime, I was out here cramped, chilly and with my eye on a bird.

Can I stop looking now?

No, he said. You must persist. These are the things you must learn to persist with.

My hip hurt. I stood up and faced him.

I am sorry but that's all the persisting I have left in me today.

We moved to the next stage of the Tall Man's training. I am not suggesting I did not appreciate or enjoy aspects of it. I am not saying that the ramifications of it were not useful and informative. I am actually not saying anything either way. I am just telling you plain and simple. There was training and I was trained. I was warned during this training. And you might say—I am certain that the Tall Man, wherever he is, will very likely be saying—I failed his training. I didn't heed the warnings. You might assume that all these words are an apology for not heeding those warnings. It might be, I am not sure. That is for you. I can only mark it here like mean cat scratches and you can let it be useful to you or not. It isn't definitive and it isn't certain. It is the very nature of warnings.

I was struggling about how to get the Glass back and what to tell the Tall Man about the Glass and how I'd left it and I knew he would tell me write it in the book. But to write it in the book I had to drive 10 miles to ▮▮▮▮▮▮▮ and that man always asks me to have tea and sit down with him and I've to be honest now . . . I didn't do it. I didn't write the explanation into the book where we were supposed to write all the explanations. And either this was how I tripped us all up or it was a combination of this and the Mole ▮▮▮▮▮▮ reporting our activities to someone.

What I did instead was I bought another glass. I went to Dunnes and I bought a glass that I thought had the look of the Glass. I put it inside a carrier bag and I planned to add a pair of latex gloves I'd lift from someone who had a box of them in their house. I was waiting to spy a box. I wasn't going to buy a whole box of latex gloves when I only needed the one pair.

I don't recall too much more on the Glass.

Because Phil wrote her explanation on the paper
And because the Glass was there in the bag

Along with the latex gloves

I was scuppered.

I might also have left something more inside the bag

And it was technically the thing in there that they techni-cally caught me for.

And maybe it was deliberate that I put it in the bag.

I didn't tell her straight.

I just said when she mentioned the Glass that I had another glass since, and that she'd find something inside the Glass in that bag. I said if it's useful just say the word when you are ready and we will do what has to be done. Other than that, I don't want any more talk about it.

You're a good woman Bina, she said. You were the only person who made any sense that time when they put me in the hospital after I lost Jimmy. I never forgot how good you were to me and I never will.

Go way, I said. It was nothing, if I had been trapped in there you'd have done the same for me.

What she did forget was to say no more about it.

The hardest thing humans have to do is say no more about it.

Phil was wrong.

Even me, I cannot stop saying no more about this.

And I won't shut up.

She chose to go.
That's one thing
But she left explanations
Accidental explanations.
That wasn't helpful
That was wrong.
She should not have gone
Because she couldn't go without explanations.

Those left behind will want explanations.

Should you not go until no explanations are needed?
Or should the explanation-hungry get over themselves?
Like myself.
Should I give up on explanations?
And have I?
Do I?
Will you?
We're not there yet.
Are we?

We'll go to the grave hoping for explanations.

We'll look at the letterbox way beyond what the postal service could ever deliver. The letter or card the person never wrote.

We look at it on Sundays, hoping for news.

I am still looking at my letterbox

But now I am watching the Tablet

Hoping for word from/of Phil and worried that Eddie could come back.

See how it is

Those we want shut of, linger.

Those who should remain, don't.

And even if you're shut of those you want gone, they still linger

And in the same way, those who do not remain more than linger

They become even more than they were.

Which was never their intention.

It's a funny old muddle

And it's why I can now only lie down.

Only lie down in the stew of it

Rather than be carrying on and rushing about trying to get past it all.

It'll never be passed.

It's how it is.

You'll never be shut of the troublemakers

And you'll never get past the loss of those you actually love

And who are useful.

Nothing to be done

The useless remain.

Only lie here and wallow in the disaster that we create.

The ones we work hard to create.

And the ones we disastrously try to understand.

Nothing to understand,

Nothing to be understood.

That's a warning and a remarking

Just as I promised.

I am good this way

I don't make promises I won't keep

And I won't shut up til I am ready

And I may never be ready

At this rate

We'll never reach the red dot

But I'll pop it here as a marker

A reminder

That it's coming.

I have begun to have my doubts.

He never stalled.

He was in and he was out.

●

Or

Bina began to have her doubts.
He never stalled.
The Tall Man was in and he was out.

●

I still can't decide how I am to tell you this
(and I continually forget what I have told you).

Eddie took things from my kitchen.
I gradually noticed them gone.
Strange things
Surprising things he'd have no use for
Wherever he is.
Like my meat pounder
And the bottle of salad cream.

Eddie had started to say he had diabetes, to compete with
Phil
And so I wouldn't kick him out.

If you've diabetes, go to the doctor and get it checked,
I told him

I'm weeing all the time, he said

You're weeing all the time on account of the drink.

No, it's not the drink, he said

The drink is nothing got to do with it

It's my accident, he said.

His accident was the code word for

Do not challenge me.

But I wasn't finished with him yet.

I have a few questions about your accident, now that you
bring it up, I said.

And not long til I didn't see him for the dust.

I did have questions

And they weren't just about the accident.

They were about other strange things in the locality that
were worrying me and more besides me.

Someone is robbing houses, I said. We are going to have
to set up a neighbourhood watch. It will be easy to catch the
person, I said, as they are a pure eejit and have no clue what
they are doing.

Travellers, he said

It's not Travellers, I said. Travellers aren't this stupid if they
are going after something.

Whoever did this is as thick as a post. Only a matter of
time til he's caught.

But we have a surprise planned for him.

Might be a woman, he said

I gave him a look

That would wither him.

The Crusties are very keen to make an emergency-evacuation plan for me. They keep saying mad things like: We might need to get you to Wales, Bina. How are you in small boats? Do you get seasick? We have a safehouse ready in Wales.

Lookit here, I tell them. Stop all this mad talk. The only way I would go to Wales is on a coach. I'm not sailing from here in a boat and you're acting like I'm an IRA man on the run, and I am not. I'm just a woman lying down. I only want to be left in peace. I don't want to go to Wales.

And it never goes very well from there, the conversation.

You can lie down in Wales, they say.

I prefer it when they leave me out.

Carry on with your plans, I tell them

I've things to do and a pan to boil.

Goodnight now.

One of the Crusties is perpetually talking about Bolivarians.

I don't like the sound of it.

I am a woman who likes a clean pair of socks

A folded towel.

I like the kettle boiled

I like a good bit of peace

I never intended to end up in such a situation as this.

I'd tell you I don't know how it happened, except I am here telling you exactly how it happened.

What makes even less sense is how I invited all this trouble into my own lap. That's the question I'd ask the Bolivarians.[55]

They say they want to bring a woman to visit me and would that be alright?

They say she's Human Rights and might help me

I say unless she is useful, she shouldn't bother coming

They ask me to define useful and this is the thing with Crusties and all their defining. Now I have an awful headache. Define that amongst yourselves. I'm going to bed.

I have done things people asked me to do because they need or needed doing.

I was not supposed to do those things.

---

[55] I'm very talented at inviting trouble upon myself. This is a warning. Get a hobby so your hands are kept busy & away from all invitations.

I have lost all my courage now.
It is a shame that.

Courage can be lost.
It can be beaten out of you.
It's a shame that.

There's probably a voice somewhere among you parping,
only if you let them, Bina
That is rubbish.
You might not let them
But life will beat the courage out of you
While emboldening the chancers like Eddie.
The chancers will always rise again.
That's a warning.
Almost a command.

That's what's created the embezzlers.
They have stored up all the courage beaten and suctioned
from those around them.
I see their kissers all over the papers.
They never put their heads down when photographed
Because they never go to prison.
Why would they go to prison when they can run away to
New Jersey and hide behind a gate?
That's what Phil said about embezzlers.

That's what Phil said about Eddie.

He's gone to Canada to hide in a whorehouse, but even the whores will have a pain in their hole listening to him, and he'll be back. You'll see.

They're working women, I said, not whores. I'm exceedingly grateful to them.

Give over Bina, she said.

●

Bina didn't like it when Phil said
Eddie would be back.
She did not like the words Eddie and back.

She doesn't want him back, ever.

●

How do you stop someone coming back, though?
More precisely, how do you stop a man coming back?

A man bigger than you.
A man you are afraid of.

●

That was another question Bina asked Phil.
And it was a question Phil asked Bina.
How do you know?
Let those who want to be gone, be gone, Phil said to Bina
In the hopes that those you don't want to come back, won't.
It was a hint
Clearly.

Phil was bold this way
The way she'd take words and lace them up
Backwards.
And she was convincing.
Because she had a big heart, Phil did.
Big strong heart in a small fraught woman.
But those were the wrong words
Wrong words, wrong thoughts, wrong sentiment.
But that wasn't why she'd have helped Phil.

Phil, though, gave her the idea

The solution

See now

If Phil was in the room

Eddie couldn't be in the room

As there was no room in the bed for two bodies.

She'd put Phil in the room

As the means to Eddie never coming back.

That was her plan

That was the plan she had gone to tell Phil the morning she found her.

●

I even bought a new mattress
And pillows
I had the clean sheets ready to go on the bed.
I was keeping them warm in the hot press.
If I'd put them on before I'd left
Maybe Phil wouldn't be gone.

●

These are the nonsense questions Bina sometimes asks
herself.

What if?
Why didn't she?
How could she?

What Bina knows is that when a person has had enough
There's nothing to make them stay
Even if you are there
Holding the sign that says, No.
Even if you threaten to arrest them
They'll just go all the faster.
Because even though Bina knows Phil was wrong
She had promised that when Phil said she'd had enough,
she would believe her.
She does believe her
She just doesn't want to

She wants to tell her that she hadn't had enough
Not yet.
But Bina knows that's all wrong.

●

I hadn't had enough of Phil
That was the trouble
I had had enough of Eddie
But not Phil
And that's why I believe that Phil was wrong
I also believe Eddie was wrong
Eddie should have wanted to be gone
Because no one wants Eddie to stay.

Bina pauses.

She contemplates whether if now, over there, in Canada, wherever he is, whoever is suffering him, there's someone who wants him to stay.

And in the same way as she cannot see that Phil had had enough, she cannot conceive that anyone would want Eddie near them. Because he's awful. Unremittingly so. Consistently.

In this regard, there's no distance between those two dots.

They are both red.

Red dots.

Who is gone

And who stays.

Unresolvable

Big red dots.

INDEX OF WARNINGS

If you ever see a person lying in a ditch, drive straight past them as fast as you can.

He might not be a nice lad.

She might not be a nice woman.

If a man comes to your door, do not open it.[56]

Old women have more to do than stand around.

Do not give a lend of your bread knife.

Do not open your hearth.

Do not open your heart.

Do not believe the common declaration: All he/she needs is a bang on the head.

———————————

[56] Unless it's David Bowie.

Leave the man on the mat.

Don't do the things you're not supposed to do.

Say No.

Practise saying No.

Do not borrow a handkerchief

Watch your phone.

Careful on the internets.

Watch your phone, did I already say that one? If so I'm saying it twice.

Say what should have been said, even after the fact. (From here to there.)

Watch the language

Pay attention to the letters (Scrabble)

People might ask you to do difficult things.

Always have a chat to yourself.

A chat can put a stop to it.

Weather can surprise you!

Write it down. All of it. Record it the way I am doing for you.

If you cannot remember, write it down, then tell someone where it is written down if you cannot remember where.

Do not write down unnecessary explanations about the things you do not want people to know. This is a bad idea.

Do not talk to the papers, even if it is just a survey on smoking.

Listen out for warnings in people's remarkings.

Write down the names of people saying clever things on the radio.

Keep an eye open for spies.

Don't make a decision if the tea does not taste right.

They need a warrant to search your house.

You'll never be shut of the troublemakers.

You never get past the loss of those you actually love.

Troublemakers do not need a warrant to ruin your life.

Chancers are hard to put down.

You might not read a word I've written here.

You'll know when you've had enough.

In
Loving
Memory
of
Carol Mary Critchley

Acknowledgements

I most gratefully acknowledge the support of the Canada Council for the Arts, the BC Arts Council and The Writers Trust Woodcock Fund, the Writers Union, and the many libraries, writers' festivals, universities and communities who have hosted readings—as well as every reader who ever read one of my books. I am immensely appreciative of your engagement with my work.

Thank you: Thalia Field, mighty first reader, epic writer, and brilliant friend.

Thank you: to Lynn Henry for such dedication and patience, Kelly Hill for the genius cover design, Emily Donaldson for the copy edit + laughter, Rick, Trish + Sharon for all else. To Alba Ziegler-Bailey, Sarah Chalfant, Ekin Oklap at the Wylie Agency in London for daily, and sometimes hourly, support, and the most intelligent and insightful readings of my work. To Eimear McBride, Rachel Cusk, Eden Robinson for reading *Bina* and offering the warmest of words and giving me courage. To Arabella Campbell for the photos. Thanks for helpful discussions: Dr. Sue Hughson, Shanaaz Gokool, Margaret McPhee (RIP), and my fellow volunteer witnesses in the Vancouver Chapter of Dying with Dignity. Thank you, also, Dr Zareena Abidin for natter and badminton.

To Dan Wells at Biblioasis for continuing to be the most decent of human beings. To the Simon Fraser University English Department for letting me teach a course in Experimental Fiction.

Bina is a novel about friendship—specifically, female friendship. I am extremely blessed to have women friends in various time zones who are far too good to me. Go raibh míle to Edel Connor, Cathy Dillon, Niamh + Grace Barrett and Mary McCarthy. For literary companionship during the long, difficult periods of writing any book, many thanks to Yewande Omotoso, Sinéad Gleeson, Doireann Ní Ghríofa, Joanna Walsh, Greg McCormick and Marina Roy. Acá en Canada gracias a mi hermana porteña Anabella Forte, hermano Fouad Matar, beloved amiga Julie Okot Bitek, Marina Roy, GJ, and my Irish gang here in Vancouver, Ita, Tara, Tracey, Siobhán, Alison, Joan et al. To Suzu Matsuda + Larry Cohen, who continuously love and support my son. To my mother, Hannah, who is the greatest of storytellers herself, + my sister, who owns the best greyhounds in Dublin. I owe much to so many; therefore, if you are reading this, consider yourself among the thanked.

The original idea for *Bina* came from a mention of her in a review of my first novel *Malarky* by the Irish journalist Joanne Hayden.

Thank you to the many healthcare workers, palliative nurses, social workers and doctors who provide care and dignity for the dying and those suffering. To all those brave souls who fought tough legal cases that led to the MAID program in Canada. For more information about MAID in Canada, please visit: https://www.dyingwithdignity.ca

Finally merci a million to my lovely son, Cúán Isamu, who uses too much electricity, cooks a mean chilli and is a great laugh. Mo cheol thú!

ANAKANA SCHOFIELD is the author of the acclaimed, Giller Prize–shortlisted novel *Martin John* (2015), which was also a finalist for the Ethel Wilson Fiction Prize, the Goldsmiths Prize in the UK, a *New York Times* Editors' Choice, and named a best book of the year by the *Wall Street Journal, The Globe and Mail, National Post, Sunday Business Post, Toronto Star,* and *The Irish Times,* among others. Her debut novel *Malarky* (2012) won the Amazon.ca First Novel Award, the Debut-Litzer Prize for Fiction in the United States, and was a finalist for the Ethel Wilson Fiction Prize. Her writing and reviews have appeared in *The Guardian, The Irish Times, The Globe and Mail, National Post, London Review of Books* blog, and *The Long Gaze Back: An Anthology of Irish Women Writers.* She lives in Vancouver, British Columbia.